MARCUS NICKLIN was born in 1931, educated at Yeovil School, completed National Service in the RAF and trained for the Anglican Ministry at the London College of Divinity (now St John's College, Nottingham). He was ordained in 1955 and served in both parish and non-parochial spheres. These included ten years as a full-time psychiatric hospital chaplain, two years training ordinands, and six years with the Children's Society. During his period as a psychiatric hospital chaplain, he completed the Birmingham University Diploma in Pastoral Studies with its training in social work, and gained an MA in theology. He resigned from his post in an Anglican team ministry in 1987. He then obtained a post as a social worker in the Employment Rehabilitation Service, assisting unemployed men and women with disabilities to regain their confidence and secure a new career. He was received into the Roman Catholic Church at Easter 1990. He is now retired.

And So To Rome

An Evangelical Pilgrimage

Margaret
from
Marcus

And So To Rome
An Evangelical Pilgrimage

Marcus Nicklin

with appreciation of
your friendship.

ATHENA PRESS
LONDON

ISBN: 978 1 84748 389 8

First published 2008 by
ATHENA PRESS
Queen's House, 2 Holly Road
Twickenham TW1 4EG
United Kingdom

Printed for Athena Press

Contents

Preface

Many books have been written by both Evangelicals and Roman Catholics explaining and defending their different positions. I am writing from the perspective of my own journey in faith and in the light of my theological and pastoral training and experience. As the story of a pilgrimage of faith, it begins with conversion to Christ, continuing in the Anglican ministry and leading into the renewed Roman Catholic Church.

Recent years have seen the publication of the reports of official discussions between the Church of England, Methodist and Roman Catholic Churches. No doubt these have been milestones on the road of ecumenical relations. However, there has been a dearth of literature dealing positively with the Christ-centred faith common to both Roman Catholic and Evangelical Christians. Both attach great importance to our need of conversion, a personal trust in Jesus Christ as Saviour and acceptance of him as Lord. Contributions from Evangelicals have tended to be critical of Roman Catholicism, focusing on perceived differences rather than making any constructive attempt at bridge building. Why, in this post-Vatican II era of ecumenism, has there been a silence towards Evangelicals on the part of the Roman Catholic Church? The simple answer may be that Roman Catholics are accustomed to thinking in terms of non-Catholic Churches, that is, denominations. Consequently, Evangelicals are lumped together with the rest of non-Catholics. Those Roman Catholics with knowledge of mainland Europe may think of 'Evangelical' in the German sense, meaning Lutheran. It may also be that from the Catholic viewpoint, it is rather like trying to get hold of jelly! For Evangelicals cannot be identified with any one denomination; indeed they sometimes take pride in professing themselves as primarily 'interdenominational'. Those who profess conversion to Christ through Evangelical preaching are likely to be advised to join a local church seen to conform to Evangelical principles. In practice, that may be either an Evangelical-Anglican, Baptist, Pentecostal-Assembly or 'house church', depending on whatever is regarded as the most 'sound' and 'live' in the locality. The Roman Catholic Church is likely to be regarded with suspicion!

Why focus on the relationship between Roman Catholics and Evangelicals? Leaving aside my own background and interest, there are three good reasons. Firstly, Evangelicals see themselves as the true successors of the Protestant Reformers and consequently of unadulterated Christianity. Secondly, the Evangelical-Charismatic churches are reputedly the fastest growing of any strand of Christianity today. Therefore, on numbers alone, they can hardly be ignored by the largest Christian denomination, the Roman Catholic Church. There is, in my view, a third reason. It is time that Christians from 'both camps' recognised the common faith they share.

It is easy to dismiss all Evangelical Christians as 'fundamentalists' and consider the discussion closed. Evangelicalism is a theological outlook that crosses denominational boundaries and comprises considerable variations. At one extreme are the fundamentalists, who refuse to accept as authentically Christian those who do not share their particular interpretation of scripture. At the other end of the spectrum are loyal members of mainstream Churches, whose first priority is a commitment to Evangelism and who work to help others respond to Christ in personal faith. Their Christian faith is Bible-based but not confined in a narrow straightjacket. They usually emphasise liturgical simplicity and informality. Even when dealing with such an 'interdenominational' movement as Evangelicalism, denominational differences cannot be ignored. Historical factors alone cannot account for the differences that (for example) exist between Evangelical Baptists and Evangelical Anglicans. My aim is to concentrate on what is common to such different Christians and to assess whether this common core of gospel-faith corresponds to the central beliefs of Roman Catholics today. As a former Evangelical Anglican, it is inevitable that I present Evangelicalism from that perspective. I regret having to employ the 'ism' syllable in describing various groupings; this is for lack of a better alternative!

I must express my indebtedness to all who have contributed to my personal development over the years, especially the members of my family, to Fr Christopher O'Brien, who received me into the Roman Catholic Church, and to my wife for encouraging me to complete this book. My thanks are also due to the members of Athena Press for their many helpful suggestions and creative presentation.

Introduction

No one has perfect parents. However great the love offered by the best of parents, they still make mistakes as they struggle to provide a secure upbringing for their children. Why, then, should it be otherwise with those who struggle to present the Good News of Jesus Christ to us, our spiritual parents? As St Paul put it: 'We are only the earthenware jars that hold this treasure.'[1] As I look back on those whom God used to bring me to personal faith in Christ, this could quite respectfully be said of them. They have been the clay pots through which I have come to glimpse the treasure of the Risen Christ.

Yeovil Parish Church in the 1940s with its tradition of 'High Matins' and choir worship was, to me, as dull and lifeless as clay! Nevertheless, there and in like parishes I became familiar with the Prayer Book and was introduced to those great scriptural hymns of the Church, Benedictus and Magnificat. However, it is to 'Crusaders' that I still look back as the context in which Jesus Christ became real to me. Introduced by a Methodist friend to that teenage boys' Bible class, with its Baptist leader and members from various Churches and none, Crusaders became an important part of my teenage years. There were football, cricket, tennis and various social activities, but at its heart was the Sunday afternoon Bible class, meeting in a Scout hut, a clay pot indeed. The Bible became a living book, the Word of God. Above all came the assurance that Jesus Christ, who had sacrificed himself for each of us, is alive and close at hand!

It was not only the dusty Scout hut that made Crusaders

a 'clay pot'. There were aspects of the culture (beliefs and ideas) accompanying that presentation of Christian faith that were less helpful. Two or three examples may illustrate this. All the members of that growing Crusader branch attended single-sex grammar or private schools. Crusaders reinforced that segregation, and accompanying the segregated ethos was a slightly gnostic attitude to sexuality. It would be grossly unfair to say that sex and sin were equated, but there was a tendency to hint in that direction. The other target for specialist treatment was the Roman Catholic Church. The latter was seen as corrupt and on no account to be tangled with. Again, in fairness, it must be said that we are speaking of the pre-Vatican II Church, and many of the items singled out as 'abominations' have now passed into history. In common with the general Evangelical culture of those days, Crusaders tended to discourage too great an involvement in the 'world'. Although this was intended to keep members from what Roman Catholics then described as 'occasions of sin', this attitude led to an opting-out of the world of social and political action. Perhaps in this respect, Crusaders and Evangelicals generally had more in common with the fortress culture of the pre-Vatican II Catholic Church than was realised! I hardly need remind fellow Roman Catholics that St Paul, when he wrote about 'earthenware pots', was addressing part of the Catholic Church. Catholics today accept the Second Vatican Council as a 'spring clean' of the earthenware pot, in a worldwide sense. Of course, even from the 'clay pot' of the pre-Vatican II Church, the glory of Christ shone. Catholics, who, as children, were brought up in the Church of that time, tell of their fear on entering the dark confession boxes. Despite that off-putting environment, they learned to love the Lord.

In the far-off days of 1948 (the year I left school), the BBC used to broadcast a Sunday evening service. It was transmitted on the Home Service, now Radio 4. From time to time, the Evening Service of Benediction would be broadcast from a Roman Catholic Church. I recall one such broadcast, when the priest preached the most powerful sermon on conversion that I had ever heard on the radio. The same Good News that had so recently become real to me through Crusaders was now coming from that 'corrupt' Church! How could this happen? That question was to remain an enigma for many years. If only St Paul's words about 'clay-pots' had been more familiar. Before leaving this matter of earthenware, let me add a further comment from my Anglican experience. My college followed the strict discipline of the daily offices of morning and evening prayer. Through regular recitation of the Psalter, the psalms became familiar. The sixteenth century language of the Prayer Book seemed almost as archaic as Latin, but that clay pot discipline introduced me to the psalms, which are so full of the emotional stuff of human life: love, hate, trust in God, bitterness about the state of the world, depression, and even paranoia, are all to be found there.

The zeal of the convert is notorious for its intolerance! Having become a Roman Catholic after many years as an active Anglican, it would be tempting to see nothing good in the Church from which I have crossed. Although I have some critical things to say about the Church of England, I wish to be fair, and I have no desire to throw out the baby with the bathwater. There is much that the Church of England believes and practises that is exemplary, and I'm not thinking of 'good taste'! Examples that spring to mind are the many conscientious pastors, devoted and active members of congregations with whom I have worked, and the frontier ministry of hospital and industrial chaplains. In the latter field, the Church of England has often led the way in trying to bridge the gulf between religion and everyday working life. For their pains, industrial chaplains have sometimes been marginalised and devalued by the stalwarts of the parochial system.

It is said that the days of the Reformation are over and that we are in the time of Reconciliation. That is music to the ears of those who remember the 'old days' before Vatican II. While every Christian should rejoice at the new spirit and changed attitudes, there can be no papering over the cracks. There are real differences to be overcome and important questions of belief to be addressed. Words are one important means of human communication. Words, whether spoken or written, can lead to faulty communication and misunderstanding. Modern psychology, psychiatry and ethology have heightened our awareness of this danger. The Churches have not been immune from breakdowns in communication. Some, perhaps many, of our differences can be accounted for in this way. But there can be no shortcuts, no question of being economical with the truth, if that truth really is the revealed Word of God. The basic problem is whether our understanding of that 'Word' is sound, or overlaid with others' misinterpretations.

My approach is that of a former Anglican with an Evangelical outlook. I naturally hope this work will be of interest to a wide readership. Many of the questions addressed will be of particular concern to those Christians who describe themselves as Evangelical. As this work stems from one person's pilgrimage, it cannot claim to discuss all possible controversial questions; there is inevitably an element of selection. Having said that, I hope the reader will find the approach reasonably objective and fair. It is written following years of work and experience based upon theological, pastoral and social-work training. From the Roman Catholic viewpoint I have tried wherever possible to refer readers to responsible statements by Catholic theologians. As far as I am aware, what follows accords with the official teaching of the Roman Catholic Church, although responsibility for what is written is mine alone. The work is offered not in a contentious spirit but in the hope that it may provoke further honest thinking and an open-mindedness freed from the shackles of past prejudice.

Notes

[1] 2 Corinthians 4:7 *Jerusalem Bible*, Darton, Longman & Todd

Conversion

The memorable Sunday evening broadcast in 1948, already mentioned in the Introduction, signalled that the Roman Catholic Church was as concerned with personal conversion as any live Evangelical congregation. The post-war years were an age when the preaching of conversion was seen as the acid test of soundness, over against the mediocre, non-enthusiastic tone of so much Anglican churchmanship. Within a very few years, England was to see the launch of the Billy Graham Crusades. The Charismatic Movement, as we know it, had not yet touched the mainstream Churches; the 'gifts of the Spirit', such as 'speaking in tongues', were as yet confined to the Pentecostal sects. The term 'born again' was sometimes used to describe conversion, but (in this country at least) it had not degenerated into the North American cliché so common today. In those immediate post-war years, the conversion to Christ of England's people was seen by Evangelicals (and indeed by a growing number of others hesitant to bear the Evangelical label) as paramount. What was to become of the Peace? How were we to persuade people to stir from their apathy to active Christian faith and return to Church?

Against this background, many men (myself among them) felt called to serve in the Ministry of the Church of England. After National Service in the RAF, I went on to train at the London College of Divinity (later to become St John's College, Nottingham). There we were given a thorough grounding in biblical theology. The College motto – 'Woe am I if I do not preach the Gospel' – was not only instilled but practised as we launched enthusiastically into College Missions. It would be wrong to create the impression that we were encouraged to present superficial appeals to 'turn to Christ'. Our appeal was based upon solid biblical teaching that opened up the scriptures as a living contemporary message. It is not difficult to see how for men trained in this tradition, the main objectives following ordination would be, firstly, a preaching and personal ministry aiming to bring people to personal faith in Christ, and secondly, to build up the spiritual life of the local congregation so that it could become a more effective evangelising centre.

In my own case, a growing involvement with men and women in various kinds of life crisis (bereavement and mental illness to name but two) created a nagging sense of the inadequacy of our training. I had not been taught to listen, or indeed any of the skills so necessary to counselling and casework. Involvement with mental health problems, both in my family and the parish, proved a baptism of fire! I return to this 'other side of the gospel coin' in a later chapter. The present concern is conversion in the Roman Catholic Church and the Churches of the Reformation.

Roman Catholics use the term 'conversion' in different ways. Those members of the Church, who, like myself, become Catholics, are often referred to as 'converts'. Clearly that is not the meaning of the word as understood by Evangelicals! Because Roman Catholic teaching emphasises the reality of God's grace sharing the risen life of Jesus with us in our Baptism, Evangelicals often overlook that this emphasis on baptismal grace is set in the context of the Covenant Community, and that the Church demands a faith response to the Covenant. The New Catechism[1] makes this clear:

'The question is how can the child receive the sign of conversion and faith while it is still incapable of conversion … The answer is that it receives the sign in the way in which it lives – in dependence on adults. Christ made his salvation a community matter, a social thing. He did not give it to individuals in isolation from each other but to a people … We bring the child into the circle of our own faith, into the Faith of the Church … The Church asks for a guarantee of Christian education.'

It has been a great joy to witness small children being baptised during Sunday Mass, and their practising Catholic parents being reminded: 'You are the first teachers of this child.'

In my experience, the Church of England, and perhaps other Churches that practise infant Baptism, have lost sight of the Christian Church as the Community of Faith. In reaction to this woolliness, many Evangelicals become Baptists. During my years in Anglican parish ministry, I worked hard preparing parents for the Baptism of their children. In the team ministry of which I was a member, we involved members of our congregations in Baptism preparation. Church of England clergy who take seriously this part of their ministry often face considerable public criticism, together with a lack of episcopal and institutional support. That Church's concept of itself as the Church of the total population takes precedence over proper preparation for the sign of entry into Christian faith and the Christian community.

I understand Evangelical apprehension regarding the danger of thinking of infant Baptism as a kind of magic rite, for I have shared that concern. I have to say, however, that there have been times when I have thanked God for the fact of my Baptism, even though I cannot consciously recall the event! For that act of grace stands, even when faith has faltered. When I have tried to explain the meaning of infant

Baptism to parents, I have sometimes compared the sacrament to a priceless cheque which has to be cashed for its value to be realised. I still believe (as a Roman Catholic) that the analogy holds true.

The necessity of personal faith in Jesus is constantly stressed in the Roman Catholic Church, and no apology is offered for using the term 'conversion' to describe our turning to the Lord. There is also, in Catholic practice, a call to continued repentance, a daily turning to Christ. Whenever this takes the form of a 'step' towards the Lord, it is sometimes described as conversion. If there is any difference of understanding between Catholics and Evangelicals, it lies here. Evangelicals confine 'conversion' to a one-off experience, usually (although in fairness not always) seen as dramatic. Roman Catholics, however, while in no way denying the reality of the 'dramatic', simply do not confine conversion to a once-for-all-time event.

In the Bible, conversion means a change of mind, leading to a change of direction, a turning to the Lord. St Paul's experience on the Damascus road is the classic example. Another well-known story often taken as the basis of Evangelical sermons is that of the 'Prodigal' son. Soon after my reception into the Roman Catholic Church, we had a parish mission. There was no connection between the two events! Over the years, I had heard horror stories of the hellfire sermons associated with Catholic missions, so I was naturally curious. At one of the midweek evening services during our mission, the mission priest preached a powerful sermon on the return of the 'Prodigal'. It was a message that would have stirred the hearts of the most Protestant of Evangelical Christians. The one possible difference in emphasis (although this may be nit-picking) was the preacher's emphasis upon the prodigality of the father in the story, and the graphic picture this presents of the love and accepting grace of God offered to us so freely. There is a

Catholic hymn which echoes this: 'The love I have for you, my Lord, is only a shadow of your love for me … My own belief in you, my Lord, is only a shadow of your faith in me; your deep and lasting faith.'[2]

Conversion has sometimes been presented as demanding humiliation, a crushing of God-given personality. In the Roman Catholic Church today, conversion is understood as the rediscovery of a sense of self-worth – because each of us is of great value to the Lord.

Emilie Griffin, telling of her own conversion experience and that of Thomas Merton, says: 'I think that for converts – indeed for all Christians – the acknowledgement of sin is not self-hatred at all, but the beginning of self-acceptance and (in the healthy sense) of self-love.'[3] In her book *How God Became Real*, Emilie Griffin describes her experience of becoming a believing Christian, being baptised in the US Episcopal Church and subsequently becoming a Roman Catholic. She says: 'By conversion I mean the discovery that God is real. It is the perception that this real God loves us personally and acts mercifully and justly towards each of us. Conversion is the direct experience of the saving power of God … Conversion is an inner change of heart, not an outward change of allegiance.'[4]

She has had to grapple in both mind and heart with conversion as a unique experience and also as process: 'There is first conversion, that upheaval in our minds and hearts which we resolve when we first acknowledge the Lord and give ourselves to him. Beyond that first conversion – as many converts learn to their surprise – there is another turning which is to last our whole life long … Some call it sanctification, growing in holiness.'[5]

Some members of Christian Churches shrink from any idea of intimacy with God, having been brought up to think of God as 'distant' and 'wholly other'. Providing we keep before us the vision of the Lord as holy, and resist the temptation to mould God into our own reflection, we can rightly think of conversion as trusting Jesus Christ as our friend and brother. The letter to the Hebrews clearly portrays Jesus the eternal-high-priest as our brother, sharing our weaknesses. Both Evangelicals and Roman Catholics are frequently reminded of Christ's own assurance: 'I call you friends.'[6] There is a popular Evangelical hymn, 'What a Friend we have in Jesus', which I first learned in Crusaders. The modern language of the Catholic Mass speaks with equal simplicity and clarity of our friendship with the Lord.

Conversion is essentially about the response of an individual man or woman to Jesus Christ. Hans Kung, however, speaks of the 'conversion of the Church'. He puts it in this way: 'We can say with joy that this conversion began decisively for the Catholic Church with the Second Vatican Council. This Church of Vatican II has renounced the siege mentality and triumphalism. It sees itself once again as the people of God on pilgrimage striding through the darkness of bondage and error to the Kingdom of God in constant need of renewal until made perfect.'[7]

I was particularly struck by this description of the experience of Vatican II as 'conversion', for it seemed to justify my own changed perception. In the light of that conversion, I have to raise the question: is it not time for the Church of England, and other Churches, to experience a conversion of comparable order? Hans Kung seems to think so, for he adds: 'Which other Church would have been able to achieve anything like Vatican II achieved? ... People respect a Church which not only preaches metanoia (conversion) to others, but practises it herself.'[8]

Notes

[1] *A New Catechism (The Catholic Faith for Adults)*, Search Press, Eighth Impression 1980, p.250

[2] *Hymns Old & New*, No. 536, Kevin Mayhew Ltd, 1991

[3] Griffin, Emilie, *How God Became Real: An Experience of Conversion*, Sheldon Press, 1981, p.111

[4] Ibid., pp.15, 21

[5] Ibid., pp.29–30

[6] St John's Gospel 15:15, *Jerusalem Bible*, Darton, Longman & Todd

[7] Kung, Hans, *Truthfulness*, Sheed & Ward, 1968, p.47

[8] Ibid., pp.169, 173

History Reassessed

There are moments of illumination in our lives. I am not thinking now of those phenomena we think of as mystical or spiritual experiences. I have in mind those insights we often preface with, 'When the penny dropped', or of which we ask ourselves, 'Why didn't I see that so clearly before?' One such instance occurred when I was initiated into the social work and psychiatric practice of taking a 'Social History'. I suddenly realised that each of us has a 'history'; and history, therefore, is not something impersonal and remote from real-life emotional interaction. Now this penny-dropping experience of mine may make me appear naive to those who learned this truth about history earlier in life or who always knew this. I can only ask such readers to ascribe it to my late development!

The purpose of this preamble is that it leads into my reconsideration of the English Reformation, and in particular the establishment of the Church of England as a national Church. There is nothing to be gained by repeating the historical facts of the period, for historians have dealt with these at length. My aim is simply to show how I, as an Evangelical Anglican, became convinced through a recon-sideration of history that I should take a fresh look at the Roman Catholic Church. I now believe that the seeds of this change were sown long before, but could only come to fruition when the climate and environment were right.

On the eve of my ordination as a deacon in the Church of England in September 1955, I and my fellow ordinands were informed that the following morning we should be swearing an oath of allegiance to the Queen. Although I realised I was to be admitted to the ministry in the established Church, I could not recall this 'oath' having been mentioned before. What troubled me was not that I was a subversive, for I had taken a similar oath on entering the RAF. My concern was that I, as a Christian minister, should be required to take this oath. What if the Queen (or more likely her Ministers of State) were to require me to follow a policy that conflicted with my conscientious allegiance to Christ? With the wisdom of hindsight, I wonder how I could ever have taken such a step! On reflection, the explanation lies in the fact that I felt genuinely called to ministry, was a convinced Episcopalian, but unable in conscience at that time to join the pre-Vatican II Roman Catholic Church. I then accepted the explanation that the oath was just a formality. Whether that makes sense to others is not for me to judge. The fact is, despite the nagging doubt, reinforced by the gowned and wigged figure of the Diocesan Registrar, I took the oath. I now believe firmly that no Christian minister should take such a step. Nor do I find convincing the explanation offered by Archbishop Robert Runcie: 'The Queen's position in the life of our Church is very much a symbolic position. She is, as it were, a chief layperson.'[1] I believe Enoch Powell was closer to the truth when he said in parliament: 'The Church is the Church of England because of royal supremacy, because there is royal – and that is to say lay – supremacy.'[2] More recently, during the course of a BBC Radio 4 debate on 'Disestablishment of the Church of England', Tony Benn went to the heart of the matter when he said: 'Church of England bishops, on their appointment, make an act of homage to the monarch, recognising the Crown as the source of spiritual as well as of temporal authority.'

In this matter of royal supremacy, the politicians demonstrate a clearer understanding than the Archbishop.

Archbishop Cranmer's homily at the coronation of Edward VI is significant in this respect. 'Your majesty is God's vice-regent and Christ's vicar within your own dominions and to see with your predecessor Josiah, God truly worshipped, and idolatry destroyed, the tyranny of the bishops of Rome banished from your subjects, and images removed.'[3]

I had never felt at peace about the behaviour of Henry VIII in relation to the Church. In 1955 I convinced myself that he was an historical relic and the Establishment a mere formality. As time passed I began to realise that my nagging doubts had a basis in reality. At that time, nearly all Diocesan bishops were ex-public school and Oxbridge, and widely regarded as 'safe men'. That was, of course, long before the battle between Margaret Thatcher and the coal miners brought certain Anglican bishops into conflict with the government. The conservative episcopal establishment came down heavily on parish clergy if they attempted to exercise any kind of spiritual discipline, such as requiring adequate preparation and instruction in Christian faith of those approaching the Church for Baptism or marriage. During my early years in parish ministry, one missionary-minded rector who initiated such practice had no less than three bishops 'on his back', demanding his resignation! From time to time I found myself in a double bind: are the Church of England bishops really acting as successors to the Apostles in spearheading the Church in its mission, or is their role that of propping up the established order?

At the end of the day I have had to look again at Henry VIII. He may well have been a man of his time bent on a male heir, but that justified neither his behaviour nor the train of events he set in motion. Even if it is true that the Pope hesitated to grant Henry his nullity decree in respect of Catherine of Aragon for fear of offending the powerful Spanish monarch, the actions of Henry and Archbishop Cranmer were not justified. There is no New Testament authorisation for a monarch to be 'head' of the Church. Clearly, religion and politics intertwined at that time. It is commonly argued by Church historians that the burning of Protestants under Queen Mary sprang from religious bigotry, but that the torture and killing of Roman Catholics under Elizabeth I was a political matter. I should not wish to condone the terrible crimes of Queen Mary's reign, but neither can the barbaric behaviour of Queen Elizabeth's government be whitewashed. Can it really be believed that the torture and inhumane execution of such persons as Edmund Campion and the majority of other Roman Catholics had any real political foundation? A visit to Tyburn Convent at Marble Arch, where those martyrs are commemorated, can put the record straight. The fact is that Queen Elizabeth and her Protestant government claimed to be more genuinely Christian than their predecessors. Had England become a genuinely reformed Christian state, such terrible acts could never have been perpetrated.

The later persecution of the early Quakers throws light on the intolerant belief system of the newly established Church. Those early Quakers may have shaken the religious reactionaries, but by no stretch of the imagination could they be seen as a political threat. During the BBC Radio debate on disestablishment already mentioned, Peter Cornwell, a former Anglican and now a Roman Catholic, said: 'The Establishment has meant rejection and persecution and has only become benign since the seventeenth century.' May it be that the neglect by the Church of England of the spiritual discipline prescribed by its own rubrics[4] has been motivated as much by corporate guilt for the dark crimes of its own history as from its declared pastoral concern for all in the land? It is widely known that guilt presents in all kinds of devious ways in the lives of individuals. However, we are only slowly becoming aware of the effects of corporate guilt resulting from the crimes of powerful institutions, such as those perpetrated during the Second World War.

The enthronement of Dr George Carey as Archbishop of Canterbury in 1991 provoked a surprising degree of interest from the media, considering the level of indifference to church-based Christianity in England. I was glad that it was George Carey who had been appointed, but the ceremonial, together with the negative criticism directed at him by sections of the Church of England, made me glad to be no longer part of the Established Church. The enthronement served to underline the Church's marriage to the State – 'by law Established' – and to remind me of my own entry to its ministry in 1955. The obsession of the Church of England with 'good taste' was also evident in the petty criticism of the new archbishop for including contemporary Christian music.

A distinguishing feature of the Church of England is the sense of 'Englishness' which pervades it. It is not too great an exaggeration to describe this spirit as nationalism. Critics may retort that the Catholic Church has, at times, and in some places, also become so closely allied with a particular nation as to appear equally nationalistic, as, for instance, in the Irish Republic. However, even if and when the Catholic Church and a country's national interests have become closely identified, there has been a marked difference from the spirit that pervades the Church of England. In the Roman Catholic Church, in whatever country, there is always the sense of belonging to the supranational Church, and that is of first importance.

The Church of Jesus Christ is, and must be seen to be, international – or rather supranational. The notion of Establishment confines a Church to becoming the religious face of that nation – a kind of totem. The term 'Church of' is in itself a denial of the 'Catholic' Church. I find it curious that the main obstacle to reunion today is seen by some

Anglicans to be women's ordination. A far greater obstacle is the basic issue of the Pope's authority. Whether we are among those who praise or blame Henry for his quarrel and breach with Rome, it is high time to take a fresh look at that critical stage of our history.

Notes

[1] *The Times*, 19 April 1982 and cited by Antony Archer in *The Two Catholic Churches*, SCM Press. 1986, p.244

[2] *Hansard*, 16 July 1984, cited Ibid., p.244

[3] Duffy, Eamon, *The Stripping of the Altars*, New Haven & London. 1992, p.448

[4] For a discussion of the Rubrics in the *Book of Common Prayer*, see the next chapter.

Discipline – a Dirty Word!

Discipline is a dirty word in England today. People cannot walk the streets safely. Police forces are stretched, and police officers are themselves in danger of serious assault. Teachers are at the end of their tether through classroom stress. Driving standards are visibly deteriorating as cars flood onto the roads. All this may sound like the moaning of the middle-aged. Alas, many undisciplined drivers are middle-aged, as a trip around the M25 will soon reveal. This is not another plea for a return to Victorian values, but it can hardly be disputed that there has been a marked change in patterns of English social behaviour indicative of a move away from discipline.

During the post-war years, the vast majority of young men were subjected to the compulsory external discipline of National Service. Students of both sexes in colleges experienced a discipline that was the same in kind, even if more relaxed in degree, as that they had known in school. My own theological college in the 1950s was run like an adult boarding school; by the 1970s it seemed like bedlam in comparison!

In this climate it is therefore hardly surprising that the Roman Catholic Church is singled out as being too strict and legalistic. How often have I heard it said, 'If you are a Catholic, you have to go to Church!' True, Sunday Mass is an obligation and I believe (on scriptural grounds) rightly so. Evangelical Christians often assert that the only valid form of discipline is self-discipline, and quote in support of this view St Paul's teaching that self-control is a fruit of the

Spirit. The Roman Catholic Church also believes this and stresses the importance of individual conscience. A careful reading of the New Testament, however, reveals this to be only one side of the coin. In the New Testament records, we glimpse the Christian community exercising a discipline over all its members. Time and time again we find St Paul rebuking Church members for breaches of Christian standards, the most glaring case being that of the man who was excommunicated from the Church in Corinth (1 Corinthians 5). Neither can it be said that the Apostles were concerned only with sexual sin. The hypocrisy of Ananias and Sapphira was dealt with even more severely! (Acts 5) Looking at discipline in the New Testament Church more positively, the report in Acts chapters 15 and 16 of the Jerusalem council is particularly significant. All members of the Church are expected, in disputed matters of Christian faith, to accept the agreed decisions of the Apostles and the leaders they have appointed.

Following the English Reformation, the Church of England attempted to administer some kind of discipline. Not only were people fined for non-attendance at church, more significantly, the rubrics of the *Book of Common Prayer* (1662) published clear rules regarding attendance at Holy Communion. These are to be found immediately before and after the rite of Holy Communion in the Prayer Book: 'Every Parishioner shall communicate at the least three times in the year... If any be an open and notorious evil liver, or have done any wrong to his neighbours by word or deed ... the Curate shall call him and advertise him that he presume not to come to the Lord's Table until he have openly declared himself to have truly repented and amended his life ... The same order shall the Curate use with those betwixt whom he perceiveth malice and hatred to reign.'[1] The language is quaint to modern ears, but the Prayer Book still has legal authority in the Church of

England and is widely used. When twentieth-century clergy have attempted to apply this discipline in the parishes, they themselves have been cast in the role of harsh wrongdoers! No doubt these rules fell into disuse as the Holy Communion became neglected and devalued. As the sacrament assumed a more prominent position again, following the Evangelical Revival and nineteenth-century Oxford Movement, the associated discipline was quietly left to history. It is not difficult to understand the reasons. The Church of England, as the Established Church, has an inbuilt sense of responsibility for every resident in England. It has also had to come to terms with 'drift'. The decline in church attendance accelerated rapidly with the Industrial Revolution and the accompanying changes in social structure. This decline was hardly surprising, considering the Church's general failure to identify with the poor and oppressed in the nineteenth century, siding instead with the rich and the powerful. It is the weakness of national Churches to succumb to the pressures of the age. A recent example is the shift in the Church's marriage discipline. Until the 1960s (when divorce was still uncommon), the Church of England followed a strict policy of forbidding the remarriage of divorced persons in church. Thirty years later we find the same Church permitting the practice – or at least turning a blind eye without too many questions being asked. It is sometimes said that the Church of England has the strictest marriage discipline of any denomination. In practice, when it comes to remarriage in church, standards differ depending upon the convictions of individual parish clergy. This means that, at best, they follow their own conscience and, at worst, the social pressures exerted by their parishioners. This somewhat capricious practice is in sharp contrast with the Catholic nullity discipline. Although the latter is often treated with disdain by Anglicans, it is a carefully regulated discipline involving the most thorough investigation of the relevant circumstances. We are into a sensitive area, but it is the inconsistencies of Anglican practice that concern me. This is especially so when we recall that thirty years ago the divorced were not allowed to receive Communion.

It is important in this context, and for the sake of truth, to pay closer attention to Catholic marriage discipline.

I served as a member of a team ministry, several of whose members were extremely critical of the Roman Catholic Church for granting marriage annulments which my former colleagues described as 'Catholic divorce'. They spoke from ignorance, for they had neither first-hand experience of the process nor had they received any accurate information. So what is the truth regarding this aspect of Catholic marriage discipline?

The Church believes marriage is a sacrament and, as Christ teaches, to be lifelong. When a case is brought to the Tribunal by one or both marriage partners, the question to be resolved is whether that relationship was a valid and genuine Christian sacramental marriage in the first instance. To reach a resolution, the tribunal examines the roots of the relationship from courtship through engagement, to the wedding and beyond.

The process is extremely thorough, and inevitably prolonged. The initial interview may run to several hours; in one case known to me, the applicant went through a five-hour interview with intense questioning. A case then goes through a number of stages, including witness interviews, and before two panels of judges. This in-depth process is a very different matter from that of the vicar of an Anglican parish making a decision whether a remarriage may or may not take place in church.

Those who have experienced this seemingly daunting process have often found that it has brought profound healing, clearing the mind and conscience of lingering doubts and conflicts, and allowing a person to come to terms with his or her past.

For fuller information, I would refer readers to Bishop Geoffrey Robinson's authoritative book.[2]

In his play *Racing Demon*, David Hare examines the dynamics of a Church of England team ministry in action. Before writing his play, the author interviewed members of the Church, clergy and laity, with the result that the drama comes close to real life in a poignant way. The approaches of the various members of the clergy team to their over-whelming and frustrating mission, leads to one member being scapegoated as the cause of failure. I suggest that the breakdown of spiritual discipline in the Church of England in general has led to a projection of failure onto its clergy. One instance is the frequent lament, 'People don't come to church because of the vicar!' Another and even more destructive example can be the treatment afforded clergy whose marriages run into trouble. Readers may recall the comparatively recent prosecution of a Sussex incumbent in an Ecclesiastical Court on charges of adultery. Why a clergyman, and why was it felt that this alleged sin alone merited such disciplinary action? In the light of the neglected Prayer Book rubrics, with their great stress upon 'sins of the spirit' and genuine love on the part of all 'parishioners', it does smack of throwing the first stone! In referring to the case, I do not intend any judgement as to the truth or otherwise of the allegations. My concern is with the false premise of singling out the clergy and of focusing on one area only of their behaviour. In this respect, the Church of England is out of step with the gospel. To the possible counter-charge that the Roman Catholic Church makes a distinction between its clergy and laity, I can only state that the Catholic Church exercises discipline over all its members. The inconsistency of the Church of England regarding the case cited is apparent in that no comparable action is taken against clergymen who practise homosexual acts. The treatment in their case appears to be a polite request to abstain, with an assurance there will be no witch-hunt!

A further inconsistency in the discipline of the Church of England, although of a different order, lies in adherence to fundamental Christian belief. Every clergyman is required to publicly affirm his or her acceptance of the Creeds. Despite this, a number of clergy deny the actual Resurrection of Jesus, as the BBC picked up in its *Heart of the Matter* programme at Easter 1992. How can the Anglican bishops permit such doublethink?

The fear of many Christians in England is that if the Church becomes too assertive and makes demands (that is the meaning of Christian discipline) people will be 'put off'. This apprehension is understandable but largely unjustified. After all, Christ made, and makes, demands of those considering discipleship. Today, as in New Testament times, some will be 'put off'. The experience of widely differing Christian communities shows that when demands are genuinely made for Christ and in real love, many respect this and respond. The name of the late Dr Martyn Lloyd-Jones, who was minister of Westminster Chapel, will be remembered by many Evangelical Christians of my generation. In his day he exercised a powerful biblical-preaching ministry, which not only packed Westminster Chapel regularly but also influenced many to deeper thought and reflection in Christian discipleship. As a twentieth-century puritan-evangelical, he had little time for either Charismatics or the Roman Catholic Church! However, he had some salutary theological insights to offer the Church of England. On one occasion in response to an Evangelical Anglican assertion that the C of E's doctrine of the Church is soundly scriptural, Dr Lloyd-Jones directed attention to Article 19 of the 39 Articles. This states: 'The visible Church of Christ is a congregation of faithful men, in the which the pure Word of God is preached and the Sacraments be duly administered.'[3] This definition, asserted Dr Lloyd-Jones, is inadequate; it should add: 'and where a godly discipline is administered!' The 'godly discipline' at Westminster Chapel was not 'off-putting' – the crowds responded.

More recently, some Baptist Churches have seen the introduction of the 'Church Restoration Movement'. I had the opportunity of observing the growth (and problems) of one such congregation. This 'Movement' introduced a discipline which extended even to the detailed direction of members' personal budgets, a discipline which (in the words of one Roman Catholic priest) 'is even tighter than ours!' I do not applaud the harsh destructive system that evolved, but simply wish to point out, in its initial and more moderate stages, the demands actually attracted new members to a fast-growing Church.

The notion that English people are all per se members of the Church of England is a myth that clouds the judgement of the Established Church to the realities of life in Britain today. In Anglican eyes, all parishioners (in practice that means residents) have 'rights to rites' in the Established Church. Few questions are raised regarding parishioners' 'duties'; to do this is believed to be rejecting.

Those who take this view would do well to reflect upon the place of genuine caring discipline in family life. If a family is to maintain its integrity and unity, there must be boundaries or limits to the conduct of its members. If the Christian Church is a large family, a comparable loving discipline is an essential part of its community life. If the underlying model of the Church is that of a national totem, then the concept of family flies out of the window. In using 'family' as a model of the Church, I do not intend it in an exclusive sense, as of a secret society behind locked doors.

The model must go hand in hand with mission, service and a clear vision of the Kingdom of God, as in the New Testament pattern.

In the first half of the twentieth century, the Roman Catholic Church presented to the world more as a fortress than a family. Those who peered in from other Churches often saw a strange, mysterious world on the other side of Catholic Church doors. The family model was there but, like an untidy household, was overlaid by accretions; with the coming of *agiornamento*, the windows have been flung open and the clutter cleared. Prior to 1960, the Roman Catholic Church bore comparison to the stereotype Victorian family. Today, the Catholic community is more like a healthy contemporary family. It is no longer a case of 'father knows best and children should be seen (at Mass) and not heard'! As Christian parents struggle to teach and live the gospel with their children in the materialistic rat race of Western society with its accompanying temptations, they have to maintain a firm but flexible discipline based on love. Of course there are rows and arguments, guilt and apologies, differences of viewpoint; but through it all the family's unity is maintained when ultimate limits are respected.

A laissez-faire Church with no boundaries, or with limits imposed on a minority, will not command respect, for it is like a sick, chaotic family where one child is scapegoated for the family's problems and ill health.

The Lord said to the Apostles, 'What you prohibit on earth will be prohibited in heaven, and, what you permit on earth will be permitted in heaven.'[4] Permission and prohibition mean authority both to govern a community and to decide questions. The Roman Catholic Church does not set out to be a monolithic giant squeezing its members into a straight jacket. The Church struggles to take seriously this commission of the Lord.

Notes

[1] *The Book of Common Prayer*, Cambridge University Press and SPCK, pp.236, 262

[2] Robinson, Geoffrey, *Marriage, Divorce & Nullity*, Geoffrey Chapman 1984

[3] *The Book of Common Prayer*, p.619

[4] St Matthew's Gospel 18:18, *Good News Bible (Today's English Version)*, Bible Societies and Collins

The Mass – Yesterday and Today

I recall attending Latin Mass on several occasions in the 1950s. It was very much as my Evangelical mentors had warned. Apart from the audible items in Latin, with which the majority of the congregation seemed familiar, there were long periods of relative quiet, during which the priest prayed with his back towards us, and rosary beads clicked. There were 'hard-line' sermons, negative in tone, warning against heretical books and the fires of purgatory! I felt as if I were back in pre-Reformation days. Evangelical prayer meetings and the *Book of Common Prayer* seemed far removed from that scenario.

After 1955, when I entered the Church of England ministry, I lost sight of the Roman Catholic Church until, as the 1960s dawned, news filtered through of changes sweeping the Church. An Anglican man I knew, who had become a Roman Catholic in the old Latin Mass days, now left the Catholic Church, disillusioned by the reforms! That made me sit up and pay closer attention to what was happening. Then, in the late '60s and early '70s, while working in a psychiatric hospital, I and the Roman Catholic chaplain together led a weekly shared session of worship and fellowship in a Therapeutic Community. People who had regarded each other with mutual suspicion were beginning to communicate and even work together. In that secular environment it was impossible to take refuge in differing doctrinal positions. Together we were exposed to agnosticism, and the problems and pain of real life.

My first real taste of renewed Roman Catholic worship,

however, came later, when I attended the funeral mass for the child of a neighbouring family. The service impressed me as a 'model' Christian funeral. It was conducted by the same priest who, some time earlier, had published an article in the local newspaper under the heading: 'I ask my Protestant friends to forgive the sins of my Church.'

It was some years later when, no longer active in Anglican ministry, I began to attend Sunday Mass in my local Roman Catholic parish. I was half expecting to find a church filled with my stereotyped 'hard-line' Catholics, but who might have reluctantly accepted the changes. Instead, I found myself in a live Christian community which had the feel of a large family. To my surprise I felt at home almost immediately. As I came to know various members of the Catholic community, I began to appreciate that the Catholic rainbow comprised a variety of colours and was not the monochrome body I had supposed. There were the 'cradle-Catholics' and the 'convert-Catholics', but not, I hasten to add, two factions. There were people active in the causes of justice and peace, and a small number of Charismatic Christians. I heard testimonies to the saving presence of Christ that I would have associated with an Evangelical congregation. The 'convert-Catholics' were from Anglican, Baptist, and Methodist churches. Some Anglicans had come from Anglo-Catholic congregations. I found myself wondering how they felt comfortable in the Roman Catholic Church today.

I have never been a great enthusiast for church buildings in general, so many of which speak of the transcendence – the otherness – of God, and little else, or are simply functional. St Peter's Catholic Church, Bearsted, is very different. The carved figure of the crucifix is of a risen, welcoming Christ; 'Come to me,' it seems to say. The altar table, as in all Catholic churches, is the focal point. Instead of looking up, as in so many churches, we look down and meet around the Eucharistic table, not only sparing us a pain in the neck, but helping to create a real sense of community. Nothing could be further removed from the darkness and distance of the medieval church building and its copies. The Lord in the midst of his people is apparent, not only in architectural style but also in the liturgy.

A few people speak nostalgically of the old Latin, but the vast majority are at home with the earthy vernacular, and exchange the Peace with real enthusiasm. I have worshipped in a fair cross-section of Anglican churches over the years, but in none have I found the mix of devotion and freedom for small children that prevails at St Peter's on a Sunday morning. There is always a child to give a running commentary on the Mass if one were needed, and without the embarrassment suffered by parents in non-Catholic churches. On one memorable occasion, when the bell rang at the moment of consecration, a tiny child began to sing, 'Ding dong bell, pussy's in the well!' She was not hushed; there was no embarrassment, simply smiling faces. That may not be everybody's cup of tea, but it is real-life worship. The Lord is in the midst of his people and concerned with all aspects of everyday life: family problems, work, leisure, the lot. I sometimes feel the murmur and chatter of small children forms a kind of accompaniment to the melody of the liturgy. As one person commented: 'There is life here!' (And is it not the Holy Spirit who is the giver of life?) In contrast, the silence following Holy Communion is a silence to be felt, and not dissimilar in quality from that of a Quaker meeting.

If what I have described is in marked contrast to the 'good taste' that predominates in many Anglican congregations, then I must also try to build bridges. The first and most striking similarity is, of course, in the Rite itself. There is a family likeness between the shape of the Mass today and 'Rite A' of the Church of England *Alternative Service Book*

(ASB.). Although there are marked contrasts at certain points, nevertheless the two are much closer than in the 'old days'.

In many Church of England parishes also, the presiding minister at the Eucharist now faces the congregation; the bitter controversies that racked the Anglican Church in this respect now appear to have been left behind. In the Roman Catholic Church, the change of position of the presiding priest seems to have happened 'overnight'. Nor has it been simply a question of style. The change symbolises an important shift in insight. Barriers have come down, and the Lord's presence is now recognisably with his people. As Peter Hebblethwaite, commenting on the changes of the Second Vatican Council, puts it: 'The priest was no longer placed as a mediator somewhere between the congregation and God; he became more of a president of the assembly … It was not that the sense of mystery had been lost; it was rather that it had been relocated. Christ came in the midst of his people directly (according to Matthew 18:20).'[1]

It is interesting that Roman Catholics and Evangelical Anglicans, both of whom share a great concern to bring individual souls to Christ, have also shared, since Vatican II and the Evangelical Congress at Keele, a renewed sense of the worshipping community with Christ 'in the midst'. In the Catholic Church, the Mass has become much more the Eucharistic offering of the whole community. There still remains, of course, the Evangelical objection to 'the sacrifice' of the Mass, on the grounds that Jesus offered one perfect sacrifice on the Cross. This Evangelical emphasis is made explicit in the consecration prayer in the Anglican *Book of Common Prayer*. The older language that was used by some Roman Catholic apologists seemed to lend support to the Evangelical objection. The impression was sometimes created in the minds of non-Catholics that the Resurrection of Jesus was almost overlooked. We return to this important question in the following chapter. What I have experienced in the Roman Catholic Church today is a joyful celebration of the Resurrection. Calvary and the Resurrection become present in the Eucharist in a timeless way beyond my understanding but real to faith. Each person is caught up in the offering, and then sent out as a living icon of Christ in the world.

I made passing reference to the earthy vernacular of the English Mass in the Roman Catholic Church. By that, I implied that the language used is far more colloquial than that of the Anglican *Alternative Service Book*. Some voices in the Church of England have criticised the ASB on the grounds of its having departed from the 'beautiful language' of the *Book of Common Prayer*. I dread to think what those critics would make of the contemporary missal! In general, its linguistic style is much simpler than that of the ASB. There are moments when its simplicity is reminiscent of some 'family services' produced by Evangelical Anglicans.

The scripture readings in the Roman liturgy are from the *Jerusalem Bible* modern translation. The responsorial mode of saying or singing the psalm admirably fulfils the Protestant Reformers' vision of congregational participation, and surely beyond their wildest dreams. The use of an antiphon before the gospel is also worthy of attention by non-Catholics. It usually comprises a suitable sentence from scripture, preceded and followed by 'Alleluias'. Interestingly, from time to time, the sentence employed is the verse of Psalm 119, familiar to many Christians as the Scripture Union Prayer. Contemporary sermons at Mass are, more often than not, expositions of the Bible readings.

It will be evident from what has been said that there has been a rediscovery of the Ministry of the Word. The documents of the Second Vatican Council make this abundantly clear:

It follows that all the preaching of the Church, as indeed the entire Christian religion, should be nourished and ruled by sacred Scripture. In the sacred books the Father who is in heaven comes lovingly to meet his children, and talks with them. And such is the force and power of the Word of God, that it can serve the Church as her support and vigor, and the children of the Church as strength for their faith, food for the soul and lasting fount of spiritual life. Scripture verifies in the most perfect way the words: 'The Word of God is living and active' (Hebrews 4:12) and 'is able to build you up...' (Acts 20:32)[2]

This is the kind of language that, in my youth, was more likely to be heard in Evangelical circles.

Two events from my experience (distant in time) may serve to illustrate this link between Evangelicalism and the post-Vatican II Catholic Church. When I was newly ordained into the Anglican Ministry, the vicar of the parish rightly insisted on a five-minute explanation of the scripture readings as set out in the Prayer Book at mid-week Holy Communion services. At that time, the practice was virtually unknown in the Church of England. To my surprise, I discovered the same practice prevailing in my Catholic parish today, although, I hasten to add, not using the *Book of Common Prayer*! On one occasion the scripture readings at a midweek Mass recalled the incident of the poisonous snakes and brazen serpent (Numbers 21) and St John's mention of Jesus being 'lifted up' on the Cross for our healing (John 3:14). The five-minute explanation and application of these Scriptures would have been equally in place in an Evangelical church. It gave me a curious sensation of déjà vu. One further instance which may demonstrate that the Vatican II document in mind has not been shelved to collect dust, occurred on Good Friday, when the liturgy includes much scripture. After receiving Holy Communion, we were reminded that: 'We enter into communion with Christ-crucified through the Word of God as well as in Holy Communion.'

In the area of music in worship, recent years have witnessed a coming together of Roman Catholic and other Christians. Forty years ago the only hymns sung by Roman Catholics were the sound, Catholic hymns of the Westminster Hymnal to the rich harmonies of Dom Gregory Murray and Richard Terry. Today the unthinkable has happened: Evangelical choruses are heard in Catholic churches. It is also refreshing to sing some of Charles Wesley's hymns at Sunday Mass. It must not be supposed that the Catholic Church has simply 'stolen' Evangelical choruses and Protestant hymns. There are some superb modern hymns and spiritual songs set to moving tunes to be found only in Rome.

If it seems trifling with non-essentials to draw attention to these shared features, it may be worth recalling that the Methodist Church regards its hymn singing as one of the essential marks of Methodism. Hymns and songs express feelings as well as cultural values and beliefs. This shared activity in worship often outweighs the impact of dogma. If the hearty singing of hymns is a mark of Methodism, and fervent spiritual songs of Evangelicalism more generally, then this also goes for Catholicism. The singing in a Catholic church can be very moving; and not only when aroused by an old favourite such as the 'Lourdes Hymn' to Mary! For myself, and for many in my Catholic parish, one such occasion has been the depth of faith and feeling expressed on Good Friday in the Taizé Chant: 'Jesus, remember me when you come into your Kingdom.'

A common objection to Catholicism (and one I used to share) is that its worship is highly ritualised and complex. Those familiar with Church of England services sometimes speak of 'high church' Anglican parishes as being like the Roman Catholic Church. Ceremonial is thought to be the common factor. Certainly there used to be an external similarity. Whatever was true of yesteryear is not so today. To avoid becoming bogged down in detail (which would be tedious to many readers) the essential difference between the Roman Catholic Church and the average Anglo-Catholic congregation can best be described as the difference between a 'family occasion' and a 'parade'. In the Church of England there is an unwritten rule of 'doing things decently'. Consequently, whatever degree of ceremonial is employed, there is a sense of 'being on parade'. One agnostic psychiatrist I knew once cynically described the Church of England as being like a fire brigade parading ceremonially but never fighting any fires. That was a gross exaggeration but nevertheless contained a sting of truth. The culture of the Catholic Church is quite different. Even on such days as Maundy Thursday, Good Friday and Easter Vigil, when the liturgy takes a more complex form, there is a powerful feeling of 'family occasion', comparable to an extended family coming together to celebrate a birthday or anniversary – with the person present. My feeling on returning home from the lengthy liturgy of the Easter Vigil was (I noted): 'We have really celebrated the Lord's Resurrection from the darkness of death.'

Notes

[1] Hebblethwaite, Peter, *The Runaway Church*, Collins, 1975, pp.32–33
[2] Flannery, Austin, OP [ed.], *Vatican Council II – The Conciliar & Post Conciliar Documents*, Dominican Publications, Dublin & Talbot Press, Ireland, p.762

The Real Presence

In the last chapter, I tried to convey something of the changed culture of Roman Catholic worship: fresh insights, new attitudes, language, music and general feel, which have followed upon the Second Vatican Council. It will have been apparent that I only touched on the belief lying at the heart of Catholic worship, namely the Real Presence of Christ in the Eucharist. This has usually been described as 'transubstantiation'.

Christians have been sharply divided in their understanding of the Lord's Supper, the Eucharist. During the Reformation period, people were tortured and killed for either believing or denying transubstantiation. Although those terrible and intolerant times are past, it seems as though folk memories still rancour to keep alive the divisions that were created. Consequently, the Supper of the Lord has become a subject of controversy instead of the Sacrament of Unity; confusion and misunderstandings continue.

I share my own pilgrimage of faith in respect of the Eucharist, not arrogantly as a blueprint, but in the hope that others may be encouraged to ponder the meaning of this sign which the Lord has given us. I shall try to map out the path by which I have reached the point of believing the Roman Catholic understanding to accord with scripture.

As one who discovered the living Christ in an interdenominational Bible-class meeting in a Scout hut, I believed (and still believe) Christ is available to all who seek him, in any place. The problem was that I could not square this with the way in which the Roman Catholic Church seemed to confine Christ to a material tabernacle in a church building. Nor was this latter merely a subjective impression of mine. A Roman Catholic priest, ordained in the pre-Vatican II period, spoke of the Church's treating Christ as 'the prisoner of the tabernacle'.

In company with many Anglicans, I took the Eucharist seriously as 'the Lord's own service for the Lord's people on the Lord's day'. I felt uncomfortable when fellow Evangelicals marginalised Holy Communion, relegating it to the position of an appendix to other services; an optional memorial of the Lord's death. Nevertheless, I shared the strong Evangelical belief that Christ is present 'in the midst' of his people when they meet, but not in the bread! In this I followed the Church of England formularies, which view the Eucharistic bread as representing rather than being the body of Christ.

Evangelicals have stood for reality in Christian faith. They have focused on the great, saving events of Calvary and the Resurrection, and have consistently believed that, to save us, Jesus has to be both truly God and truly human. In this they are one with Roman Catholics. An Evangelical Christian's faith goes deeper than a simple acceptance of the Creed. It is a personal trust in the Risen Christ. That being the case, why do not Evangelicals believe the Real Presence of the Lord in the Eucharist? I believe the real basis of their objection goes back to the *ex opere operato* explanation of the sacraments that used to be so common in the Roman Catholic Church. This was understood by Evangelicals as debasing the sacraments into quasi-magical rites. So insistent are Evangelicals on the accessibility of the Risen Christ to the believer, that (in practice) they have tended to bypass the Eucharist in a kind of spiritual short-circuit. Evangelical reluctance to embrace the doctrine of the Real Presence demands closer attention.

It is a fact of social psychology that we humans tend to conform to the beliefs of the group in which we live, work or worship. In Evangelical culture, as in Catholicism, there is a strong tradition operating. Following the example of Archbishop Thomas Cranmer, Evangelicals are ever vigilant for signs of idolatry. When statues with lights were common focal points of prayer in Catholic churches, this suspicion was perhaps understandable. The desire by Evangelical Christians for pure spiritual religion extended to (and still extends to) the Eucharist, so that their focus is upon the unseen Risen Lord, not the Eucharistic elements. This leads Evangelicals to interpret our Lord's words of institution metaphorically. It would be wrong, therefore, to attribute Evangelical hesitation regarding the Real Presence to an inherited tradition alone.

Evangelicals stress the necessity of personal faith on the part of those coming to the sacraments. They take seriously the warnings in the New Testament to members of the Church.

St Paul, for instance, in a letter to the Church at Corinth (1 Cor. 10:1–5) reminds us how the Israelites en route to the Promised Land 'received the sacraments' yet failed to please God. The letter to the Hebrews conveys a similar call to saving faith, which was so lacking on the part of the Old Testament pilgrims (Heb. 4:1–2).

Too great an emphasis on my faith, of course, may turn my attention upon myself rather than upon the Lord who is present with us.

I suspect there may be another insidious factor influencing the Evangelical mind against the Real Presence in the Eucharist: namely the age-old pernicious influence of Gnosticism. This philosophy, which took diverse forms and caused so much trouble in the early centuries of the Church's history, holds to the view that the unseen spiritual realm is alone good, whereas the visible material world is essentially bad. Evangelicals do, of course, condemn this heresy, but overt condemnation is no guarantee of a mindset free of such sinister influence. Much of our thinking has its roots in the subconscious, or, as Carl Jung believed, in the 'Collective Unconscious'. Given this possible influence, it is not difficult to see how it could lead to the playing down of such material substances as water, bread, wine and oil as vehicles of grace and the very presence of Christ. Once free of Gnostic thinking, the opening words of St John's first letter may come alive with new meaning: '...something which has existed since the beginning, we have watched and touched with our hands: the Word who is life.' (1 John 1:1)

When I became a regular attender at Sunday Mass in the Roman Catholic parish where I then lived, I began to experience the life of the Catholic Church from inside. In the joyful, large 'family gathering' around the altar table, there was a real sense of the Risen Lord active in the midst of his people. No longer could it be said that Christ is seen as 'the prisoner of the tabernacle'. The tabernacle (in which the Blessed Sacrament is kept) is there as in every Roman Catholic church. At St Peter's it is built into the wall of warm stone behind the free-standing altar table, where the setting seems to convey a sense of a 'homely' presence of Christ. The Risen Christ is not only in our midst but remains with us when Mass ends. There we have a continuing reminder that Jesus Christ is the same, even though our feelings fluctuate, circumstances change and faith may falter. It could be said that the Roman Catholic Church makes explicit the faith expressed in the Evangelical song: 'Be still for the Presence of the Lord, the Holy One, is here.'

Some may suppose from the foregoing that this Catholic parish is in some way exceptional. Of course, Roman Catholic parishes are not identical.

However, when we turn to the introduction to *The Weekday Missal*, it is apparent that renewal in the Roman Catholic Church has not been a piecemeal affair: 'Christ is really present in the assembly itself, which is gathered in his name, in the person of the minister, in his word, and indeed substantially and unceasingly under the Eucharistic species.'[1] Clearly then, the Roman Catholic Church recognises, in company with other Christians, the Lord's presence in the midst, but also believes Christ to be substantially present under the 'bread and wine'. This last statement may well cause Evangelical eyebrows to be raised and hands to reach for Bibles!

So, what did Jesus actually say at the Last Supper to his disciples? Obviously the vast majority of English Christians have to rely on the English translations of the New Testament, and it is just here that these are inadequate to capture the full meaning of the original. St Luke tells us that Jesus took a piece of bread, gave thanks to God, broke it and gave it to them saying: 'This is my body, which is given for you. Do this in memory of me.'[2] I always used to take that to mean, 'This stands for my body broken on the Cross'. If Christ was physically present, sitting there, how could he also be 'in' the bread? My understanding fell short in two respects. Firstly, I overlooked that Jesus was anticipating his Resurrection. In the second place, I allowed the English translation 'body' to colour my thinking, instead of being open to the force of the Greek word *soma*, which itself translates the Aramaic spoken by Jesus. Hebrew, Aramaic, and Greek had no separate word for 'self'. So, in Greek the word *soma* was used to include both body and self. This becomes clearer in a sentence where St Paul uses that same word.[3] The older translations read: 'Present your bodies a living sacrifice.' Today's English version renders this as: 'Offer yourselves as a living sacrifice to God.' When, therefore, Jesus said, 'This is my body', he meant 'This is *me*; my whole self.' Keep in mind that he is anticipating not only his agonising death, but also his Resurrection.

In his encyclical letter *Mysterium Fidei* (1965), Pope Paul VI, writing of the Eucharistic presence, said: 'It is called the 'real' presence, not in an exclusive sense as though the other forms of presence were not 'real', but by reason of its excellence. It is the substantial presence by which Christ is made present without doubt.'[4] I have found the writings of Teilhard de Chardin illuminating, even if difficult to understand in places. An interpreter of Teilhard, Fr Martelet says: 'We should not try to envisage a Christ who is contained beneath the species ... Just as the risen Christ is much less contained in the world than the world is contained in him, so we may say that Christ is much less in the bread and wine than the bread and wine are in him 'converted' and changed in the newness of his life.'[5]

Another reason for my reluctance to accept the Catholic understanding of the Eucharist was the traditional Evangelical interpretation of 'Do this in memory of me', the emphasis being upon our remembering. I do not say this is wrong, but that it is an inadequate understanding of Christ's words. The Greek word used is *anamnesis*, which means 'call to mind'. But who does the 'calling to mind'? Ourselves, God or both? In the Greek translation of the Old Testament, this same word is used to describe God 'remembering'. After the flood, God says of the rainbow: 'When the rainbow appears in the clouds, I will see it and remember the everlasting covenant between me and all living beings on earth. This is the sign of the promise which I am making to all living beings.'[6]

The Dutch Catechism aptly sums up what I have tried to say, in this way:

At the last supper, Jesus already made present the sacrifice of his life. It was a prophetic action – 'an anticipatory memorial'. It was a memorial which already made the death on the Cross really present in the symbol. Friendship between the Father and us is definitively restored by this sacrifice ... To join in the celebration of Mass is to partake of this sacrifice and to be associated in the making of the covenant between God and his people. It takes place not amid the thunders of Sinai, but with the joyful and festal simplicity of bread and wine, in thanksgiving and among beloved companions ... The sacrifice has already been offered. Strictly speaking we offer no other sacrifice than the sacrifice of Christ. No other offering is demanded of us ... It was Jesus' intention to enable his disciples to make bodily contact with his sacrifice and the covenant.[7]

The more recent *Catechism of the Catholic Church* deals with this at greater length.[8] An aspect of Roman Catholic worship that has appealed to my faith, and one that has remained constant through the liturgical changes, is its objectivity. By that I mean that the focus is Christ-centred. It is Christ himself who speaks to us through the scripture readings. It is Christ's presence in the Eucharist that is primary, rather than 'my remembering'. It is this objectivity which underlies the welcome and acceptance of small children at Mass, in contrast to so many non-Catholic services, where their presence is felt as a distraction, and often resented. This objectivity is also a corrective to an unhealthy introspective spirituality. I recall an Anglican bishop comparing God to an onion! In his sermon he expounded the idea that if we strip away the layers from ourselves (as we might those of an onion), eventually we find God at the centre. Perhaps! The Real Presence of Christ in the Eucharist is a constant reminder to run the race of life 'looking to Jesus' as our point of reference, rather than our own changeable nature.

It might surprise some Evangelical preachers to discover that Holman Hunt's famous picture *The Light of the World*, which so vividly illustrates Christ seeking admission into our lives, is also used by Roman Catholics. 'Listen! I stand at the door and knock; if anyone hears my voice and opens the door, I will come into his house and eat with him, and he will eat with me.'[9] The final part is less often quoted by Evangelicals than the former. However, the last part comes alive when we hear the Risen Christ reminding a lukewarm church of his Real Presence in his Supper!

Notes

[1] *The Weekday Missal*, Collins, 1982, p.XII

[2] St Luke's Gospel 22:19, *Good News Bible (Today's English Version)*, Bible Societies and Collins

[3] Romans 12:1, *Revised Version*, Cambridge University Press and cf. *Today's English Version*, Bible Society.

[4] Cited by Michael Evans in 'Is Jesus really present in the Eucharist?' Catholic Truth Society, 1986, p.3. This brief booklet not only sets out the Catholic doctrine but also does justice to the beliefs of Calvin, Cranmer, Luther and Zwingli.

[5] Martelet, Gustave, *The Risen Christ and the Eucharistic World*, Collins, 1976, p.178

[6] Genesis 9:16, *Today's English Version*

[7] *A New Catechism: The Catholic Faith For Adults*, Search Press, pp.166, 340

[8] Chapman, Geoffrey, *Catechism of the Catholic Church*, Geoffrey Chapman, p.307 ff

[9] Revelation 3:20, *Today's English Version*

Mary

As a child I remember asking my mother: 'Who are Roman Catholics?' The question was sparked off by two children in my primary-school class who were both Roman Catholics. One amazed me by her profound understanding of sin. It came as a contribution to a child-hood discussion of violence and murder. (There really were fewer murders in those days, but when they happened they were headline news.) 'It's not only a sin to murder some-one,' my young Catholic informant pointed out. 'It's also a sin to want to kill someone!' The other childhood acquaintance was a boy whose Catholic contribution impressed me for less worthy reasons. One day he raised his hand in class and asked the teacher: 'May I go now? It's a Catholic feast day.' What sort of Church is this, I wondered, that releases you from school for feasts!

My mother's answer to my question – 'Who are Roman Catholics?' – had a deep and lasting influence. 'Roman Catholics worship the Virgin Mary!' Years later, that parental statement of belief was reinforced by the Evangelical culture in which I came to trust in Christ, and also by my first 'live' experience of Catholic worship. The first part of that evening service seemed to confirm my mother's belief. It consisted of numerous 'Hail Marys' and 'Our Fathers' recited in rapid succession, the former far outnumbering the latter. In retrospect, I recognised the Rosary. At the time, I was left with the clear impression that Mary figured as of greater importance than God. The experience seemed to corroborate the Evangelical insistence that the Catholic Church had lost sight of Christ as the one mediator between man and God. So, in the light of that, what is the role of Mary, and how have I (a convinced Evangelical Christian) come to be at home with Mary and the Catholic Church?

I think the story begins with my long familiarity with 'Magnificat', the song of Mary. The words have been familiar from childhood. Gradually, however, Mary's song has come to be more than just another item at Evening Prayer. There has been a growing sense that as we say or sing Mary's song, we do so in her company. Moreover, as I began to reflect upon the words, several things began to emerge. The opening verse has Mary trusting and rejoicing in the Lord as Saviour. As the first recorded person in the New Testament to do this, she leads the way, and so is very much the prototype Christian believer. It is totally inadequate simply to view Mary as the Messiah's physical mother – full stop. After giving birth and hearing of God's revelation to the shepherds, she responds by 'pondering and treasuring' these things in her heart.[1] Mary's response to God is both physical and spiritual, a response involving her whole being. I have come to believe that it is a sad fact that the Churches of the Reformation, while recognising Mary as mother of the Saviour, have failed to acknowledge her as the prototype disciple.

The more I thought about Magnificat, the more of a revolutionary song it appeared to be. For Mary, God is alive and active – He has scattered the arrogant; He has brought down tyrants; He has filled the hungry – hardly the lyrics of a captive wife! This strain of liberation theology clicked with me as having something to say to everyone concerned with justice and peace issues.

The emerging image of Mary grew clearer with a visit to Israel. What particularly struck me was the journey made by Mary in her early pregnancy to Elisabeth. There is now a modern tarmac road from Jerusalem to Nazareth, and we travelled by motor car. Even so, it was a journey of over sixty miles, with the risk of harassment by Israeli soldiery. Think of Mary making that hilly journey over rough roads on four-legged transport, from Nazareth to Ein Karem (the village near Jerusalem which was John the Baptist's birthplace). There was the additional hassle of the Roman troops of occupation. When Mary reached Elisabeth's home she stayed about three months, St Luke tells us (Luke 1:56), presumably to give support to the older woman, who might be having a difficult pregnancy so late in her life. I can only say – what a woman!

Non-Catholic Christians tend to say that there is not a great deal said about Mary in scripture, and certainly no mention of people praying to her. There are a number of New Testament passages that Roman Catholic writers usually quote in response. Without wishing to ignore the importance of all of them, I simply wish to share two New Testament passages in which Mary is prominent and which have become important for me.

Following the Ascension of Christ, we find Mary praying with the embryo Church. The prototype believer prays with the Church. She who bears the Word of God, the world's Saviour, prays alongside us. It may be said: 'but that was in her lifetime.' Surely Mary, as the prototype Christian is among that 'large crowd of witnesses' the writer of the letter to the Hebrews so graphically describes as cheering us on in our gruelling race (Hebrews 12:1). The crowd of supporters (who have themselves run the race) has now been enlarged and enriched by those New Testament saints who were still running as the epistle was being written.

The second key passage for me, which gives Mary a special role, is in St John's Gospel (19:26–27) where Jesus, as he hangs on the Cross, seeing the disciple he loved, says to Mary: 'He is your son', and then to the disciple, 'She is your mother.' The common interpretation of Christ's words is that in his dying agony he was simply committing his mother to the care of St John. Jesus had brothers or, if you prefer, stepbrothers. Why not leave Mary with them, if her care was his only concern? There is nothing to suggest they were the type to ditch their responsibilities! There is more to this passage than 'care'. The person selected for this filial relationship is the one representative disciple then close at hand and who really loved the Lord. The implication is that, from now on, Mary is the spiritual mother of those who love Jesus; she is the Mother of Christians, the Mother of the Church.

In the light of these insights it now seems natural to invite Mary's prayer support. Why should this seem strange to Christians who frequently ask for one another's prayers? In the 'Bidding prayers' (Intercessions) at Mass, the person leading usually invites the congregation to join in the 'Hail Mary' prayer. The invitation will often be prefaced by some such comment as: 'Let us ask Mary mother of the Church to pray with [or for] us.' In the Catholic Church there is a sense of praying not only with the others physically present, but also with those already in heaven. This comes to a climax in the Eucharistic Prayer, where we are reminded that we approach the Lord in the company of Mary, the Apostles, and all the saints and martyrs[2]. This sense of praying with Mary and with the 'crowd of witnesses' also extends to one's own prayers at home or wherever. It is not 'just me' at prayer. I hope this does not give the impression that I have some special mystical insight. What I am trying to communicate is that this experience is part of the communal shared faith of the Roman Catholic Church and, as I now believe, thoroughly scriptural.

Despite all that has been said, I have to admit that I find it difficult to pray the Rosary! It is not used publicly in my local Catholic parish, and I have no evidence of its wide use by individuals. The experience of Fr Gerard Hughes at Medjugorje during his *Walk to Jerusalem*, reassures me that my antipathy to the Rosary may not spring entirely from Protestant prejudice. Speaking from his concern for justice and peace, he says, 'I told Anita about the uneasiness I had felt during Mass and of my fear that the message of peace of Medjugorje should be lost through the enthusiasm of the rosary brigade, flocking to the place for spiritual kicks and a sight of the dancing sun, seeking a false peace which would protect them from the need to change.'[3] The Rosary can contribute to 'spiritual kicks' in much the same way as 'charismatic gifts' and large-scale Evangelical rallies, but that does not necessarily invalidate their use.

The Rosary can be a positive way of prayer, as Sister Mary Francis demonstrates in her booklet *How to Pray the Rosary*. She sees the reason for its disuse as its misuse: people 'saying it and not "praying" it'. Sister Mary sets the Mysteries of the Rosary against their scriptural background and illuminates its use with Bible-based reflections.[4]

I have written of my own developing attitude towards Mary the Mother of the Lord. Apart from brief allusions, I have not made any general reference to sources of official Catholic teaching today. For those wishing to pursue this further, I suggest the relevant sections of *Catechism of the Catholic Church* or *Mary Mother of the Redemption* by the Catholic Theologian Edward Schillebeeckx. I conclude the chapter with the following extract from the latter.

> The Church is so profoundly aware of the fact that 'Jesus' means 'Yahweh has saved' that she feels that the term 'co-redemption' might imply that Mary though subordinate to Christ, was nonetheless complementary to him in the bringing about of the Redemption. The Church is absolutely convinced of the fact that there is one and only one Mediator between the Father and us his children.[5]

He then goes on to quote a sentence from the New Testament dear to the hearts of Evangelicals: '...there is only one mediator between God and mankind, himself a man, Christ Jesus.'[6]

Notes

[1] See St Luke's Gospel 2:19, *Jerusalem Bible*

[2] A clear example is the Eucharistic Prayer for Reconciliation: 'You have gathered us here around the table of your Son, in fellowship with the Virgin Mary, Mother of God, and all the saints.' (*Parish Mass Book*, Mayhew McCrimmon, 1992 edition)

[3] Hughes, Gerard W, *Walk to Jerusalem*, Darton, Longman & Todd, 1991, p.181

[4] Francis, Sister Mary, *How to Pray the Rosary*, Mayhew McCrimmon, 1975

[5] Schillebeeckx, Edward, *Mary Mother of the Redemption*, Sheed and Ward, 1964, p.XIV and paragraph 970 of the Catechism.

[6] 1 Timothy 2:5, *Jerusalem Bible*, Darton, Longman & Todd

Peter and the Pope

Anyone familiar with the New Testament must surely agree that Simon Peter, the fisherman, is one of its most colourful characters. For many Christians, however, the apparent gap between Peter the fisherman and the Popes of the Roman Catholic Church seems something of a 'knight's move'. Forty years ago the chasm between the two, to me, appeared so wide as to be akin to two different species of animal. Despite that apparent discrepancy, however, I found it difficult to escape from the unique role Christ assigned to Peter among the twelve Apostles. The change that has taken place in the Papacy in my lifetime has to be either miracle or manipulation on an unprecedented scale. Before deciding in favour of the latter option, why not look again at Peter's role in scripture?

Time and again in the gospels, Peter is prominent among the Twelve, and almost always he appears as their spokesman. What is most significant, however, is the commission given him by Jesus and the outworking of this commission in the early Church community. Jesus had invited the disciples' response to the searching question, 'Who do people say that I am?' He received a variety of answers. It was Peter who hit the nail on the head: 'You are the Messiah, the Son of the living God!' Christ's response is significant: 'Good for you, Simon, son of John! For this truth did not come to you from any human being, but it was given to you directly by my Father in heaven. And so I tell you Peter: you are a rock, and on this rock foundation I will build my church, and not even death will ever be able to overcome it. I will give you the keys of the Kingdom of heaven; what you prohibit on earth will be prohibited in heaven, and what you permit on earth will be permitted in heaven.'[1]

I used to think of 'the rock' referred to here as that of Peter's faith in Christ. While it is absolutely true that Christ is a solid foundation for life, that is not the primary meaning of his words to Peter. Like other non-Catholics, I read significance into the slightly different words for 'rock' in the Greek New Testament. There, Peter is addressed as 'a stone' (*petros*), while 'this rock' is *petra*. It is doubtful, though, whether that distinction can be pressed. The original conversation would have taken place in Aramaic, a similar language to Hebrew, where the same word in both instance is *kepha*. Oscar Cullmann, the Protestant theologian, says: 'The solution of the Reformers, that the rock is only the faith of Peter does not satisfy ... There remains only the one possibility, that by this saying Jesus actually meant the person whom he characterised by the name 'rock' ... For this reason all Protestant interpretations that seek in one way or another to explain away the reference to Peter seem to me unsatisfactory ... The Roman Catholic exegesis must be regarded as correct when it rejects those other attempts at explanation.'[2]

To understand the meaning of 'the keys', we have to look at Isaiah (22:15–22), where God, speaking to Shebna, manager of the royal household, anticipates a future post-holder 'who will have the keys of office; what he opens no one will shut, and what he shuts no one will open.' So Jesus commits to Peter the keys of his household, installing him as manager. As Karl Rahner says: 'By receiving the keys, which designate the administrator of the house, not the porter, Peter is given power to grant admission to the future kingdom.'[3] We see Peter carrying out this awesome responsibility first on the day of Pentecost (Acts 2) and then in declaring the kingdom of God open to non-Jews (Acts 10). Peter's responsibility did not end there. The 'keys' also included authority of prohibition and permission, or, in other words, discipline in the Church community, the household of God. A telling example of Peter carrying out that function is the case of Ananias and his wife Sapphira (Acts 5). There is no reason to suppose that deceitful couple held any 'public office' in the Church. They were 'lay' members, a caution to those who accuse the Roman Catholic Church of 'legalism' and 'strictness' toward its members when it exercises discipline!

The burning question is whether Christ's commission died with Peter. It would be just as reasonable to ask: did the Church die with the Apostles? It has been argued by some Christian theologians that Jesus (in the days before his death) did not look beyond the first generation of disciples. Whether or not that is so (and the first Christians did hope for Christ's appearing in their lifetime) the Church today facing the challenges of the twenty-first century still needs a Peter!

One of the fears of non-Catholics is the folk memory of 'bad' Popes. No historian today would attempt to whitewash the dark chapters of Papal history. In this respect it is important to keep Peter himself in our sights. 'I am a sinful man, Lord!' he once said. Jesus didn't dispute that, but nevertheless accepted Peter, and not only accepted him but entrusted him with unique responsibility. Even more significant is Peter's behaviour immediately after being appointed as manager of the household. Jesus had begun to share with the Twelve how he, as Messiah, would also be the suffering servant of the Lord. This was more than the Twelve could take. Their idea was of a Messiah 'taking power', and of top jobs for themselves in the new regime. Peter, the spokesman, took the Lord on one side to 'put him right' (Matthew 16:22).

Jesus' rebuke is very strong, but he does not rescind the role assigned to Peter.

Another instance of Peter's human weakness and limitations comes to light after Christ's Resurrection. On the beach, Jesus said to Peter, 'Do you love me more than all else?' The three times repeated question and answer will be familiar, perhaps (on account of the limitations of our English language) too familiar! In the original, the question and answer were not repeated in the same form each time, for the Greek language of the New Testament uses two different words for 'love'. In order to bring out the full force of the conversation, I quote the New English Bible translation of John 21:15–17, using the footnote alternative rendering.[4] Jesus said to Simon Peter, 'Simon son of John, do you love me more than all else?' 'Yes Lord,' he answered, 'you know that I am your friend.' 'Then feed my lambs,' he said. A second time he asked, 'Simon son of John, do you love me?' 'Yes Lord, you know that I am your friend.' 'Then tend my sheep.' A third time he said, 'Simon son of John, are you my friend?' 'Lord,' he said, 'you know everything; you know that I am your friend!' Jesus said, 'Feed my sheep.'

Keeping in mind that this conversation took place on the shore alongside the fishing boat and its equipment (plus its valuable haul), it is likely that Peter is being asked whether he is prepared to give up all hope of a steady job and business prosperity in order to give himself for life to the preaching of the gospel and care of the Lord's people. It is an invitation to sacrifice. Peter's response is an ambivalent one. Friendship yes: sacrifice cannot be guaranteed. This is a man with human limitations, but an honest man, not a model of perfection. This is the man whom the Lord recommissions to take chief pastoral responsibility.

Although it is a pastoral role that is entrusted to Peter, it is important to keep in mind the biblical understanding of what this means. In scripture, shepherding involves not only care for the flock, but also responsible rule or leadership. In his chapter on Israel's 'shepherds', Ezekiel makes clear the leaders' dual function of caring and ruling. Pastoring the growing Church in the first century was no more a one-man job than in the twentieth; but it was still one person who was appointed to head it up under Christ: Peter!

There is no doubt that the office and role of the Pope is still the 'bottom line', the make-or-break point between the Roman Catholic Church and other Christian Churches. It is understandable that non-Catholics should continue to feel reticence, when haunted by the folk memory of bad Popes. Jesus himself hinted that the Apostle's successors might not be all that could be desired when he cautioned the steward-managers in St Luke's Gospel (12:42–46). Bad managers provide no justification for abolishing authorised management. Someone has to take ultimate responsibility for leadership of the community. If God-given leadership is rejected, other leadership arises. It can be more constructive to look at the implications of this issue in a 'non-Church', secular setting, free from the legacy of past controversy. I have attempted to do this from my experience in a therapeutic community, in the chapter devoted to the 'Priesthood of All Believers'.

A sticking point for non-Catholics (and which I had to work through) is the question of 'Papal Infallibility'. About this, there has been much misunderstanding. For an authoritative and readable account of this, I refer readers to the Catechism.[5] However, there are still some points to clarify here. Papal Infallibility does not mean the man cannot make mistakes. In the early years of the Church, even St Peter himself was openly opposed by St Paul for his inconsistent Christian practice (Galatians 2:11–14). Neither does Papal Infallibility mean (as some have supposed) that the Pope can add new and fanciful doctrines to the gospel revealed by Jesus Christ. The Second Vatican Council makes this quite clear: 'When the Roman Pontiff or the body of bishops together with him define a doctrine, they make the definition in conformity with revelation itself … they do not, however, admit any new public revelation as pertaining to the divine deposit of faith.'[6]

There is a sense in which Infallibility can be understood as a negative charism; that is to say, setting boundaries or limits to what is or is not to be believed as Christian truth. Although the Second Vatican Council endorsed the definition of its predecessor in regard to Papal Infallibility,[7] it also made clear that the concept must be understood in the context of the whole church and not of the Pope in isolation from the Church. 'The holy People of God shares also in Christ's prophetic office; it spreads abroad a living witness to him … The whole body of the faithful who have an anointing that comes from the holy one (cf. 1 John. 2:20 and 27) cannot err in matters of belief. This characteristic is shown in the supernatural appreciation of the faith (*sensus fidei*) of the whole people when, from the bishops to the last of the faithful, they manifest a universal consent in matters of faith and morals. (The *sensus fidei* refers to the instinctive sensitivity and discrimination which the members of the Church possess in matters of faith.)[8]

This *sensus fidei* must surely ring bells in the hearts of many non-Catholic Christians. Among Evangelicals especially, there is a kind of *sensus fidei* in their understanding of the gospel. However, it is in its outworking in, for instance, social issues that we see this breaking-down as the various Evangelical leaders (quasi-popes) command their respective followings! A recent symposium by a number of Anglican Evangelical theologians provides evidence of unity regarding the gospel, but a very different picture both with regard to the Church and to the kingdom of God in our contemporary world.[9] Two examples may serve to illustrate this. Gavin Reid in his careful analysis 'Evangelicals, the Evangel and Evangelism' says: 'While Evangelicals have clear understandings about the meaning of the evangel and evangelism, they need to recognise that evangelism in practice is a far more messy business than they often allow.'[10]

Another contributor, Vera Sinton, in her competent discussion of recent evangelical interest in social ethics, reveals the deep divergences that exist. She says: 'The interpretation of recent evangelical history outlined in this chapter is under strong attack from a new wave of evan-gelists who would see it as the period of the great evangelical sell-out. Their fears are threefold: Social concern saps energy and enthusiasm for evangelism. The complexity of social action undermines the simplicity of the gospel. Those who are speaking and writing on social ethics are not sufficiently biblical.'[11]

I must make it clear that this is not Vera Sinton's position: she is simply bringing to light the divisions among Evangelicals. It is when confronting issues created by our highly developed and complex technological culture to which scripture provides no direct answers that Evangelicals are deeply divided. The latter may respond by pointing to differences among Roman Catholics! There is some truth in this, but the essential difference is that within Catholicism the *sensus fidei* does not fragment under the impact of contemporary issues because each local church and each individual member remains in communion with 'Peter'. The Pope – as Peter today – provides the focal point of unity and a point of final reference.

It is important to conclude this chapter by recalling that it is the Holy Spirit who guides and works through the Church in all her members. Peter Hebblethwaite reminds us of this (in relation to the Pope) when he says: 'Pope John

XXIII used to find sleep at night with the thought, "Relax, Angelo, it's not you who runs the Church, but the Holy Spirit!" '[12]

Notes

[1] St Matthew 16:15–19, *Good News Bible (Today's English Version)*, Bible Societies and Collins

[2] Cullmann, Oscar, *Peter: Disciple, Apostle, Martyr*, SCM Press, 1953, pp.206–207

[3] Rahner, Karl, *Foundations of Christian Faith: An Introduction to the Idea of Christianity*, Darton, Longman & Todd, 1978, p.334

[4] St John 21:15–17, *New English Bible* [Footnote], Oxford University Press and Cambridge University Press

[5] Chapman, Geoffrey, OP, *Catechism of the Catholic Church*, Cassell & Co, pp.206–207

[6] Flannery, Austin, [ed.], *Vatican Council II, The Conciliar & Post-Conciliar Documents*, Dominican Publications, Dublin & Talbot Press, Ireland, pp.380–381

[7] Ibid., p.380

[8] Ibid., p.363

[9] Tinker, Melvin, [ed.], *Restoring the Vision – Anglican Evangelicals Speak Out*, MARC 1990

[10] Ibid., p.90

[11] Ibid., p.144–145

[12] Hebblethwaite, Peter, *The Runaway Church*, Collins, 1975, p.240

Priesthood of All Believers

When I was newly ordained as an Anglican curate in 1955 and attended my first meeting of a Parochial Church Council, I received a shock. In my ignorance I had supposed that the vicar 'ran the parish', backed up and supported by the active laity, and the PCC in particular. Although the parish I served as assistant curate was considered a happy one, the strident voices and bickering had to be heard to be believed. The vicar in question was a saintly man and a good chairman. Having come under Quaker influence, he worked hard to achieve consensus in PCC meetings and so avoid an aggrieved minority. Sadly, he was up against Church of England 'democracy' founded upon legal powers and majority votes. It was certainly a shock to a green young curate who had been naive enough to regard the Church of England as a reformed part of the 'Catholic' Church, governed by bishops and presbyters.

I have always been grateful to the late Roderick Carter for teaching me to work towards consensus in meetings and so cause the least hurt and injury to those present. Years later, I was to experience 'consensus' in the very different context of NHS psychiatry, and to this I return presently.

It is worth reflecting on what the outcome might have been if Jesus had asked the disciples to vote on whether he should face crucifixion. It is because there is a givenness about the Christian gospel that we do not find a democratic church in the New Testament. The priesthood of all believers is fundamental, but we see there a Church under the leadership of the Apostles or their appointed representatives.

The Evangelical reader in particular may well wonder what this reference to democracy has to do with what (s)he understands by the 'priesthood of all believers'. I can only beg the patient indulgence of those readers. The traditional Evangelical view of the Priesthood of All Believers has developed in reaction to the idea of a mediating priesthood coming between the believer and God. Each Christian believer, it is affirmed, has direct access to God through Christ the one High Priest. Today, the Roman Catholic Church affirms this as clearly as any other Christian body. This is demonstrated by the repositioning of the presiding priest at Mass! What is questionable is whether Evangelicals, and indeed other Christians, have fully explored the meaning of the Priesthood of All Believers in terms of its scriptural usage and its implications in the real world. In thinking about this important belief, we cannot evade such issues as democracy in Church government, if only because the Priesthood of All Believers has sometimes been confused with Church democracy.

For me, the Priesthood of All Believers really came alive while serving as a full-time psychiatric hospital chaplain. Christians often forget that there are times when God speaks to us from the world outside, in the way that in Old Testament days God acted through a pagan ruler such as Cyrus (Isaiah 45:1). Our society has tended to reject mental illness as something outside 'normal' experience, having nothing to teach the 'sane' majority. Perhaps attitudes are slowly changing as people become more aware of the stresses in modern life and that one person in ten is likely to require psychiatric help at some point in their lives. In terms of my own personal development, the decade I spent working in the psychiatric area of the NHS proved significant.

It was my privilege to work with, and under the guidance of, a very experienced and progressive Christian psychiatrist, the late Dr James Mathers. He was the last medical super-intendent of Rubery Hospital, Birmingham, and as such he led the hospital out of a repressive pyramidal power structure to something approaching a Therapeutic Community. When James Mathers took over responsibility, the medical superintendent was akin to an ultramontane pope. He 'held the keys' in both literal and metaphorical senses. Prior to Dr Mathers' incumbency, many abuses had occurred within the hospital regime. James Mathers took up the reins of power as a 'good pope', a reforming leader who set in motion a process of renewal. Locked doors were opened; patients began to be seen as disturbed and damaged human beings in need of understanding and no longer as inmates to be controlled by a regimented system of harsh repression.

The model which replaced the repressive system of locked doors and physical restraint was the 'Therapeutic Community'. The Therapeutic Community model of management in psychiatry evolved during and after the Second World War, but built on older foundations. Although it developed within the secular psychiatric context as a milieu in which people with mental health difficulties might find wholeness, its origins can be traced to Christian sources.[1] The Therapeutic Community model is worthy of careful consideration by the Christian Churches for more compelling reasons than that of historical interest. Therapeutic Communities have had to work through many problems comparable to those facing Christian Churches and the Catholic Church in particular. Among these have been problems of hierarchy, authority, structure and suppressed 'lay' potential. Before trying to assess the significance of this process for Christian communities, it may be as well to define 'Therapeutic Community'.

Dr Maxwell Jones, who redeveloped Dingleton Hospital at Melrose along Therapeutic Community lines, described the Therapeutic Community as 'one in which a conscious effort is made to employ all the staff and patient potential in an overall treatment programme, according to the capacities and training of each individual member.'[2] Should this sound rather abstract, it may be more interesting to describe how these Therapeutic Community principles worked out in one unit on the Rubery campus in Birmingham. This was the John Conolly Hospital (named after a pioneer reforming nineteenth-century psychiatrist). The 'John Conolly' accommodated ninety inpatients together with a number of day patients. Its staff was headed up by a medical director and two consultant psychiatrists, together with a nursing director and nursing staff, a social worker and administrative staff, making up a considerable hierarchy. There was a daily Community Meeting, which everyone was expected to attend (in Catholic terminology, an obligation). The staff wore no distinctive uniform, and at the Community Meeting everyone sat 'in the round', forming two large concentric circles. This meeting of the whole Community was followed by a series of therapeutic groups, staff and ward meetings. Each meeting had a life and agenda of its own but was under obligation to 'feed back' to the large Community Meeting. It might be supposed that the latter would be a tedious affair, full of dry reports. Far from it. The daily Community Meeting was anything but dull. Incidents that had occurred during the previous day or night were 'fed in'; incidents that were often stranger than fiction! Instant reactions could explode at any time. There was freedom of expression ranging from embarrassing confessions to verbal abuse. It was not, however, a free-for-all: there were limits; for instance, physical aggression was not permitted. There were no locked doors. But if anyone walked out of the Community Meeting, (s)he was expected to give a satisfactory explanation or be brought back.

This 'permitting' or 'forbidding' of certain types of behaviour was significant. It was said and believed that the

Community set these limits. While this was true in the sense that the entire Community discussed the outworking of the rules, it was less obvious that the hierarchy was ultimately responsible for initiating and overseeing this discipline. In other words, the 'permitters' had not abandoned their role, even though they now involved the whole Community in a degree of shared responsibility. If, for example, someone flouted an accepted norm that consequently affected or diminished the life of the Community, the Community Meeting would be made aware, if only to ensure the person was not being scapegoated. However, it was the psychiatrist (entrusted with the legal power of 'the keys') who then carried out the discipline of discharging that patient from the caring community. (The close parallel with the discipline of excommunication, or perhaps temporary suspension from communion, will be apparent.)

Hierarchy had been 'flattened' in the sense of no longer operating in the authoritarian manner so characteristic of traditional mental hospitals. Hierarchy was less prominent, but nonetheless present and active. It was there because it was essential: firstly, to guarantee the transmission of received psychiatric doctrine and practice. Secondly, if the authorised and informed hierarchy had been removed by democratic vote, other leaders would have been, 'thrown up' (pardon the phrase) to satisfy every whim, or vocal element, in the Community.

In traditional psychiatry the doctor has adopted a more or less benign authoritarian approach. Put simply, it has been 'the doctor knows best' approach. That may or may not be appropriate in other fields of medicine; in psychiatry it has been seriously questioned. The 'doctor knows best' approach can be reassuring to some patients in rebuilding a sense of security. But for many it has spelt false security, for traditional doctor-dominated psychiatric practice has tended to suppress the remaining initiative of people already crushed in life. The very word 'patient' derives from Greek and implies passivity.

The Therapeutic Community refuses to acknowledge patients as passive recipients of treatment. They are seen as real human beings, each having a valuable contribution to make. The Community's purpose is to help each person identify the hindrances to his achieving that potential. 'What is making you feel more depressed or angry today than you were yesterday?' one patient may ask of another. 'Why does John always become angry every time Mary speaks?' a doctor or nurse may ask the Community. Taken at face value and out of context, these may seem pointless questions. In a caring community there is a fair chance of someone being able to elaborate the circumstances that surround the disturbing and painful behaviour. Sometimes the murky unresolved past is seen to be dictating present responses.

The guilt-ridden person often finds release and acceptance in the absolution of the therapeutic group. It is the kind of acceptance demonstrated by Jesus in the gospel, when he calls not the self-righteous but sinners to change of mind. The interactions of such a Therapeutic Community form part of a process of painful discovery. But it is not all pain; there is in the openness and acceptance also a great deal of support, for it is a fellowship of people who have experienced, and are experiencing, failure as well as beginning to discover new purpose in life. The members of the flattened hierarchy are there, as part of the Community. They are 'participant observers' keeping the ship on course, setting limits when things become too painful or destructive, and absorbing criticism for their efforts!

Mention has been made of 'consensus'. It is important to return to this concept, not least to avoid the false impression of a body of highly suggestible people being manipulated by a sophisticated leadership. Staff successfully avoided this trap most of the time, for they were disciplined participant-observers. Whatever the group, what was paramount was the 'feel of the meeting'. (Quaker readers will at once be on this wavelength.) There was no formal voting; there were no majority decisions. Issues were talked through, often painfully, and sometimes following periods of silence. The feelings of silent minorities were opened up and examined. Attempts at avoidance of painful areas were probed. There were no anaesthetics to ease the pain of the process, such as glib reassurances. The one criticism that could be made might be that, in such a Therapeutic Community, truth could be taking precedence over love. Conversely, of course, love sometimes involves pain, as family members know all too well.

Every group or organisation needs some means of resolving conflicts and of decision-making. Whatever the relevance of either authoritarianism or democratic decision making by majority vote to other spheres of life, both are alien to the Therapeutic Community and to the Community of the Church. There is an interesting comment on the life of the early Christian community, in the Acts of the Apostles: 'The group of believers was one in mind and heart.'[3] The experience of both the Quakers and the secular psychiatric Therapeutic Community demonstrate to the Churches that it is not necessary to resort to the world's ways of conflict resolution.

I have described the Therapeutic Community in some detail because it can be seen as a kind of 'secular church'. It is a caring community which has developed from the power pyramid of the traditional mental hospital. It makes no claim to be a perfect society, but rather a community whose members are struggling to work through their conflicts and failures. It is a community where people learn from, and care for, each other in new ways. It is a community working through to consensus, but with a given hierarchy essential to its continuing life.

Before further consideration of the issues that are raised by Therapeutic Community principles and practice for the Christian Church, it may be wise to pause and take a mental breath! For a phenomenon such as a Therapeutic Community may be outside the experience of many readers. Moreover, our society still likes to perceive the world from a cerebral perspective and to reserve the affective, feeling side of our being to the private area.

The Therapeutic Community reflects (however imperfectly) the kind of community envisaged by St Peter and St Paul when they describe the entire Church community in terms of 'Priesthood' and the 'Body of Christ'.

It is a healthy sign that the word 'community' is beginning to replace 'congregation' in Roman Catholic parishes. 'Congregation' smacks of people sitting in straight rows and not really relating to one another; not least because in that arrangement you look at the back of the person in front! There is an absence of face-to-face meeting. Traditionalists may like it that way, but it actively discourages 'community' in the sense the New Testament understands it. Thankfully, new Roman Catholic churches are being built 'in the round'. It is a tenet of Therapeutic Communities to always meet in a large circle that may number one hundred or more people. It is interesting to observe that Quaker meeting houses are invariably set out 'in the round'. There is no doubt that the physical structure of a building affects (or reflects) the social structure of its users. Therapeutic Communities meet in the way described, to facilitate and encourage open communication. It is this open communication that we are slowly rediscovering in our churches. I recall with sadness some Anglican congregations I have visited where there has been a marked reluctance even to 'share the Peace'; and that symbolic act is but a starter. Open communication between members of a community 'oils the wheels' of genuine care for one another. It makes a greater demand than formal church attendance.

A nurse who herself became a patient in a psychiatric Therapeutic Community, commenting on her experience said: 'It was from each other that we gained most support. There was always someone to listen, whoever happened to be near when one felt distressed.' In the years before its closure, a large mental hospital in Essex was transformed by being developed along Therapeutic Community lines. Its medical superintendent, Dr Denis Martin, himself a practising Christian, wrote:

> As a Christian I ask myself, should not the Church Fellowship be a Therapeutic Community based upon the free-flow of Christian love? Should it not be providing the kind of atmosphere in which people are free to be themselves and to find healing in the redemptive nature of an accepting sacrificial love, the love of God mediated by members of the Church – To what extent do we share our real life together in our Churches? What do we do with our resentments, jealousies, ambitions, dependencies, and sexuality, in our Christian community? Do we cover them up by straining to appear good Christians, or can we really share them together and find healing in the love of God which accepts us as we are and does not demand that we just become good?[4]

When St Peter wrote: 'Let your love for each other be real and from the heart',[5] it must be love of that quality he had in mind, because he immediately went on to describe the entire Christian community as a priesthood, offering sacrifices. 'Become a holy priesthood, to offer spiritual sacrifices to God through Jesus Christ.'[6] It is tempting for Christians today to confine this offering of spiritual sacrifices to 'church work'. St Peter is addressing members of the Christian community living under the stressful social pressures of a harsh pagan society and possessing no church buildings, as we know them. The most likely meaning of spiritual sacrifices is 'acts of social service'.[7] That suggests 'practical help'. In an age without social services, that kind of spiritual sacrifice by Christians must have made considerable impact. Such sacrifices are still needed. Recently, while recovering from major surgery, I had good reason to be thankful to those who gave me practical help at considerable cost to themselves! Social workers see another dimension to this 'social service', akin to the help available in a Therapeutic Community. It is that of being 'open to' and 'accepting of' another, without expecting some personal gain.

William Barclay's comment on St Peter's letter is helpful: 'The Latin word for priest is *pontifex*, which means bridge-builder. The priest is the man who builds a bridge for others to come to God; and the Christian has the duty and privilege of bringing others to that Saviour whom he himself has found and loves. The work of each day can then be understood not just as breadwinning but bridge-building; every legitimate routine or challenging task as in some way demonstrating Christ's presence and love in the world for which he died.'[8] That was written by a late professor of the Church of Scotland. In my experience it expresses what the Roman Catholic Church understands and teaches as the responsibility of the priesthood of all the baptised. I have been struck by the way in which every new member, every candidate for Baptism and Confirmation, is anointed with oil, marking the entry of each to the Priesthood of All Believers. As the Catechism puts it: 'The whole community of believers is as such, priestly.'[9] It is interesting to observe that in Catholic churches, Communion rails have disappeared, demonstrating that every person shares the responsibility of bringing the gospel to the world.

The Roman Catholic, Carlo Carretto, of the Little

Brothers of Jesus, said: 'We are all priests, men and women alike.' He quotes with approval the stance of St Francis of Assisi: 'Francis did not want to be a priest because he had the particular charism of developing in the Church ... the priesthood of all the baptised.' He continues: 'Let us never forget; in baptism we all become priests, and from these priests, these true priests, anyone ordained by the bishop in Christ's name to serve the church is chosen ... The community has need of leaders, shepherds, heads, celebrants; and these we call the presbyters.'[10]

Although St Paul does not refer directly to the priesthood of all Christians, his model of 'the Body' as descriptive of the Christian Church certainly resembles the Therapeutic Community in the way it involves every member. It could be said that the concept of Therapeutic Community has derived from St Paul's blueprint, and in some ways is more closely followed by those psychiatrists than by the Churches! 'Now you are Christ's body,' he writes to the Christian community in the pagan Greek city of Corinth, 'and each of you a limb or organ of it.'[11] The important points to notice for our present purpose are that all the members of the body play a purposeful role in contributing to the life and functioning of the Community, but that they are not all the same: 'There are varieties of gifts, but the same Spirit. There are varieties of service, but the same Lord.'[12]

In St Paul's model, Christ is the head of the body; in this all Christians agree. But what of the skeletal structure that holds the body together and makes it possible for that body to remain and function as a unified whole and not fall apart? Could that possibly correspond to the Catholic hierarchy? It will be tempting for critics to retort that a skeleton represents death! This is true, without the rest of the bodily organs in healthy working order, not least the eyes, ears, speech and tactile sensation, all of which enable the body to relate to the world around it. It may be dangerous to press the analogy too far, but deadening for ecumenism if we refuse to consider it.

As we consider the role of hierarchy, it is relevant to recall that St Peter himself said: 'To the rest of you I say: do what the elders [presbyters] tell you...'[13] This is not an isolated quote, but just one instance of Peter and the Apostles acting on the authority given by Christ. Taken on its own, this text from St Peter's letter might suggest an authoritarian role, even verging on dictatorship. Understood in the wider context of the whole letter, which stresses the faith and mutual responsibility of all members of the Christian community, it represents a role more akin to that of the hierarchy as I have experienced it in the psychiatric Therapeutic Community.

We have seen how the hierarchy is essential to a continuing Therapeutic Community. As well as guaranteeing authentic doctrine, and so keeping the ship on course, members of the hierarchy have ultimate responsibility for what is allowed and what is forbidden within the Community. In other words, even in a 'liberal' Therapeutic Community, someone has to 'do the permitting'! In the Communities I have known, the leaders were not elected but were appointed by regular NHS procedures. The one important distinction will have been their suitability as persons to work in a non-authoritarian manner. Clearly there is a given-ness about such appointments, just as there is in that of the leadership of the Roman Catholic Church. In its secure leadership provided by the Pope presiding over bishops from many nations, the Catholic Church is supranational. It is not tied to narrow national interests and local cultural norms, as is the case with the Church of England and Orthodox Churches. It would appear, however, that one of the current tensions within the Church is between so-called 'conservative' and 'liberal' elements. Put simply (perhaps too simply), there appears to be a tug of war between the 'orders down the line' brigade and the 'let the people decide' faction! Such approaches to government and decision making, put in those terms, seem irreconcilable. My plea to both is to explore the principles of the Therapeutic Community model, so that the 'mind of the whole Church' may be better comprehended. As a Therapeutic Community-type milieu is more fully worked out at all levels, every member would be encouraged to develop and use his or her gifts without being diverted into such frustrating democratic structures as the Church of England's synods and their free-Church equivalents.

The stereotype still prevails of a Catholic parish as a priestly one-man band plus supporters. I was surprised to discover an active 'laity', a feeling of 'our' church, with teams of readers and lay-ministers of the Eucharist. We even have a church committee. Perhaps the term 'committee', with its connotations of rigged votes and frustrated and hurt minorities, should be abandoned in favour of 'working party'. The committee in question is, in practice, a working party, for it works loyally with the parish priest, free from the strictures and legal powers that bedevil so many Anglican PCCs. I am told by fellow Catholics that our parish is way ahead of many in its depth of community. This only goes to show that the Catholic Church as a whole still has a long way to go in developing Therapeutic Community practice. In this ecumenical age, the Church might do well to dialogue with the Quakers, rather than confine its contacts to the larger non-Catholic Churches.

Mention has been made of the term 'flattening of hierarchy' in relation to psychiatric Therapeutic Communities. Brief explanation is needed if this is to have any relevance to the Christian Church. In the traditional hospital, hierarchy was synonymous with power and status. The 'higher' the person was, the more power (s)he wielded. This was both symbolised and actualised by keys. All doors were locked, but there was a hierarchy of keys! Those persons at the 'top' of the hospital power-pyramid had a master key which unlocked all doors. Staff at the various lower levels had keys which opened either part of the building, such as a corridor, or simply one ward, as the case might be. At the bottom of this power structure were the patients for whom the hospital existed! After the doors were unlocked, following the reforms of 1959, the old attitudes defining status remained. This meant that consultant psychiatrists were seen not only as sources of knowledge and expertise within their field, but as having higher 'status' than other staff (who might know the patients better as people). By contrast, psychiatrists working in a Therapeutic Community sat 'in the round' with the rest. Although they were still valid authority figures, they also became more exposed and open to questioning. In this way they shared the weakness and failure of fallible humanity, as well as their knowledge and leadership.

The experience of Therapeutic Community life became, for me, a living illustration (however imperfect) of the Lord's description of his own vocation: 'The Son of Man himself did not come to be served, but to serve, and to give…'[14] Jesus gave a practical demonstration of this when he washed the disciples' feet. So, flattening of hierarchy means neither its crushing nor its removal, but the rejection of status as exemplified in the transformation of the mental hospital power-pyramid into the life-enhancing culture of the Therapeutic Community.

In the Roman Catholic Church, a dramatic process of change began with Pope John XXIII, and it continues today. Pope John described himself as 'servant of the servants of God.' That demonstrated a radical change of attitude within the Church. The problem of status, of course, is not confined to the man at the top of an organisation! It is easy for those at other levels to confuse responsible leadership with status. Pride is a besetting sin of human nature, and it is often fed by personal insecurity or other emotional damage sustained earlier in life. What has been said of organisations and their perils is applicable to all Churches.

The Churches of the Reformation (including the Church of England) sometimes take for granted that the Protestant Reformation rid their communities of institutional evil. In reality, the Reformation in no way changed authoritarian and status-seeking attitudes. Where organisational changes have taken place, the old has been replaced by other equally oppressive structures as, in the case of the Church of England, the Establishment and, more recently, the General Synod. I believe much the same could be said of the power structures of the other mainstream 'Reformed' Churches. Vatican II has been the springboard for change in the Roman Catholic Church. What evidence is there of comparable change in other Churches, including those that define themselves most clearly as 'Evangelical'?

What I find refreshing, at a time when we are surrounded by so many powerful institutions, is the renewed outlook of the Roman Catholic Church, whereby she sees her role as that of the Pilgrim People of God, committed to following the footsteps of the Crucified Lord.

I conclude this lengthy chapter on a lighter note, although not too light, for I have in mind a visit to the Albert Hall for a prom concert. In a real sense, everyone there participated. It would have been possible for each person to stand up and sing their own song. The consequences would have been constant interruptions, discordant individual noises, chaos! If that kind of behaviour had occurred, the orchestral music would have been drowned. Is that not precisely what has happened and is happening in our divided Christian Churches? The Church, like those in the Albert Hall, includes people from a variety of countries and cultural backgrounds, each eager to hear and share the music of the gospel. It, too, needs a conductor; not to write the music, for that is already completed and given, but to interpret and apply afresh the inspired score. A conductor may be good, bad or indifferent, but he is essential to the performance. Roman Catholics see the Pope as, under Christ, fulfilling that role!

Notes

[1] The Retreat, in York, founded and run by Quakers (1796), pioneered the humane treatment of the mentally ill. The author's unpublished thesis in the University of Birmingham library discusses the Therapeutic Community and its origins.

[2] Cited by Dr Denis Martin in his book *Adventure in Psychiatry*, Bruno Cassirer, 1962, p.VII

[3] Acts 3:32, *Good News Bible (Today's English Version)*, Bible Societies and Collins

[4] Martin, Denis, *The Church as a Healing Community*, Guild of Health, pp.7–9

[5] 1 Peter 1:22, *Jerusalem Bible*, Darton, Longman & Todd

[6] 1 Peter 2:5, *New English Bible*, Oxford University Press and Cambridge University Press

[7] Selwyn, E G, *The First Epistle of Peter*, Macmillan, London, 1961

[8] Barclay, William, *Daily Bible Study*, St Andrew's Press (James & Peter), p.196

[9] Chapman, Geoffrey, *Catechism of the Catholic Church*, Cassell & Co, p.346, para.1546

[10] Carretto, Carlo, *I Sought and I Found: My Experience of God and of the Church*, Darton, Longman & Todd, 1984

[11] 1 Corinthians 12:27, *New English Bible*

[12] Ibid., 1 Corinthians 12:4–5

[13] 1 Peter 5:5, *Jerusalem Bible*, Darton, Longman & Todd

[14] Ibid., Mark 10:45

Justice and Peace

There was something especially satisfying about the six years I worked with the Children's Society. During the time I was with the Society, new patterns of social work with deprived children and their families were being pioneered. It was thrilling to be in a position to relate this work to the gospel, which sets such value on each human life. At the same time it sharpened my awareness of the gap in thinking that persists in the minds of some churchgoers, and not least in a number of Evangelical Christians. Sometimes I would be asked: 'What has that aspect of the Society's work to do with the Church, or the gospel?' More pointedly, a few conservative Evangelical parishes politely showed me the door!

Some years earlier it had slowly dawned on me that there are two sides to the gospel coin – the individual and the social – and that Churches separate these at their peril. I had begun to realise that the 'Evangelical' understanding of the gospel as I had received it paid scant attention to social problems and their underlying social structures; these were not seen as pertinent to the preaching of the gospel, whose chief aim was to change individual people.

Although this was generally true of mainstream Evangelicalism, there were marked exceptions to this inadequate grasp of the gospel, notably the witness of the Salvation Army. For the majority of Evangelical Christians, however, social concern tended to be equated with 'mere humanism', and professional social work simply not understood. Sadly, this thinking still persists at the fundamentalist end of the

Evangelical spectrum. Recently an American evangelist said: 'There is no such thing as a Social Gospel. God only speaks to, and changes, individuals.'[1] I have to admit that I suffered from this kind of tunnel vision. It was as if my reading of Old Testament theology, with its call to social justice through Amos and Isaiah, lay buried, waiting to be rediscovered. James Barr, in his book on fundamentalism, makes a sweeping criticism of the attitude of conservative Evangelicals towards power and wealth in society: 'Many observers have noted the way in which fundamentalists are at home in the world of money and profit ... The acute religiosity of the fundamentalist does not alter the fact that he almost fully accepts the secular and economic structure of that world ... And the [conservative Evangelical] religion does not require or even encourage any fundamental criticism of the forces in society which provide these elements of power and wealth, opportunity and influence.'[2] In fairness, it must be said that, although James Barr's criticism is applicable to many Evangelical and Charismatic groups, there are others who now actively witness to the gospel concern for social justice. It is probably a fair estimate to say that Evangelicals in England divided in their attitude to social concern around 1970. Certainly, a noticeable change of outlook distinguishes many Anglican Evangelicals today from that described above.

In my own experience, it was exposure to social problems, especially those presenting in the area of mental health and psychiatry, that widened my vision. Supervised social-work placements in Birmingham introduced me to inner-city poverty and problems on a scale that I had hitherto relegated to a bygone age.

The greatest challenge to the gospel's relevance came from the psychiatric hospital and those it served. In particular, how could the Good News of Redemption and Forgiveness become reality for patients suffering severe mental health problems, and for those responsible for their care? Psychiatric patients were not so many 'islands' of humanity. Whether or not they had families, they were all affected by the social situation in which they found themselves. If that was stimulating and genuinely caring, they began to find new meaning in a grey world. So much depended upon the attitudes of carers and visitors – how they viewed the 'patient'. Is (s)he seen as 'not quite human' or as a person of value? I served in the hospital during a period when immense changes of attitude towards people with mental health problems were being implemented. The 'locked door' regime had gone, only vestiges remaining, and 'inmates' were being treated as patients; as men and women with genuine health problems. In this context the conversation recorded in St Matthew's Gospel[3] becomes contemporary: 'I was a stranger and you made me welcome; sick and you visited me.' 'Lord, when did we see you a stranger and make you welcome ... sick and go to see you?'

The late Dr Bob Lambourne (psychiatrist and theologian) used to speak of the 'sacrament of the cup of cold water' to describe time spent with those for whom words no longer conveyed meaning. It is not hard to see how such attitudes can begin to change the social environment – such as that of a hospital.

However, this is not a treatise on the gospel and social justice, but the story of my journey as an Evangelical Christian to Rome. The question remains: how does this discovery of both sides of the 'gospel coin' relate to my becoming a Roman Catholic? When I began to worship with the Catholic congregation in Bearsted, I discovered that Justice and Peace issues were being taken seriously. I became aware of an active Justice and Peace group; although 'group' is a misnomer, for that suggests a separate cell. The Justice and Peace group functions as a kind of 'heart', circulating awareness of Justice and Peace issues throughout the whole body of the local Catholic community. The whole body, in turn, responds by generously supporting such projects as a shelter for London's homeless, a 'Third World' parish in Nicaragua, as well as the work of CAFOD, to name but three. I began to discover that Justice and Peace groups are now part of the life of Catholic parishes. Underlying this concern is the Lord's word: '...whenever you did this for one of the least important of these ... you did it for me.'[4] For the Roman Catholic Church today, then, social needs and issues are not an optional extra but a response to Christ in the poor and oppressed.

It would be wrong to imply or infer that the Church has only just discovered this gospel teaching! In 1891 Pope Leo XIII issued his Encyclical, 'Rerum Novarum'. Among other important issues, this laid down the rights of workers to a just wage, the limitation of working hours, and the right to form trade unions; this at a time when these human rights were being fought for and hotly contested by the wealthy and privileged, and when the major non-Catholic Churches in England were (by and large) on the 'wrong side'!

On 1 May 1991, Pope John Paul II issued an Encyclical marking the centenary of 'Rerum Novarum'. This letter, entitled 'Centesimus Annus', not only recommends a re-reading of the older Encyclical, but also invites us to look seriously at today's Justice and Peace issues. It is only possible here to refer briefly to some of those mentioned. Pope John Paul refers to 'the still largely unsolved problem of the foreign debt of the poorer countries'. He goes on: 'Equally worrying is the ecological question which accompanies the problem of consumerism and which is closely connected with it.'[5]

Speaking of modern warfare, Pope John Paul says: 'I myself, on the occasion of the recent tragic war in the Persian Gulf, repeated the cry – "Never again War!" No, never again war, which destroys the lives of innocent people, teaches how to kill, throws into upheaval even the lives of those who do the killing and leaves behind a trail of resentment and hatred, thus making it all the more difficult to find a just solution of the very problems which provoked the war.'[6]

After noting that at the root of war there are usually such real grievances as injustice, poverty and exploitation, the Pope goes on to say that the poor need to be provided with realistic opportunities. 'Creating such conditions calls for a concerted worldwide effort to promote development, an effort which also involves sacrificing the positions of income and power enjoyed by the more developed economies. This may mean making important changes in established lifestyles, in order to limit the waste of environmental and human resources, thus enabling every individual and all the peoples of the earth to have a sufficient share of those resources.'[7]

Despite the social teaching of the Catholic Church, I suspect there are many Christians who feel uneasy when it comes to working out the gospel's implications in the world of politics, business, commerce and social policy. In this country we have grown accustomed to confining Christian faith to 'Church matters' and to the private domestic area of life. This may be one reason why *Honest to God* caused such a storm when it was published. I have no idea what influence, if any, the author (the late Bishop John Robinson) has had upon the Roman Catholic Church. His *Honest to God* certainly made me think again, in particular his use of the phrase 'the Holy in the common' with reference to the Eucharist. 'The purpose of worship is not to retire from the secular into the department of the religious ... but to open oneself to the meeting of the Christ in the common. The function of worship is to focus, sharpen and deepen our response to the world and to other people beyond the point of liking and self-interest...'[8] He continues: 'The test of worship is how far it makes us more sensitive to "the beyond in our midst", to the Christ in the hungry, the naked, the homeless and the prisoner.'[9]

It can come as a surprise to notice how much of Jesus' time was spent in the 'common', secular area of life. His background in carpentry is familiar. Less familiar is the Galilee of the first century, which features so much in the gospels. For most people Galilee is a place of tourism and pilgrimage. For Peter and the others it represented 'work'. Despite my theological training, the full impact of this only struck me during a seminar with industrial chaplains. The Anglican industrial chaplains (a bit like the French worker-priests) have had to work out the meaning of Christian faith in the world of factory and business. They have helped us see that, far from being a quiet area of retreat, Galilee was a hub of industry and commerce. How significant then, that after the Resurrection it was to Galilee that the disciples were directed, to meet the Risen Christ? (Matthew 28:10). Those first disciples would not have been surprised by the Galilee rendezvous, even though we might have expected it to be the temple! They had been so accustomed to hearing Jesus teaching there, about the kingdom of God, meaning the rule of God in every department of life. It was in Galilee that Jesus had used Peter's 'office' – his boat! In Galilee the 'social problem' of the hungry 5,000 had been brought to Jesus' attention. In Galilee there took place the first encounters with the agents of political power of that time. Even the Upper Room venue for the intimate communion with Christ at the Last Supper was followed immediately by their 'going out' to the Garden and Calvary. It was outside, in the 'real world' of power seeking, politics and scape-goating, that Jesus was crucified. So there is no escape from the context in which the first disciples understood their Christian responsibility.

In our day, the media focuses all too often upon the

alleged shortcomings of the Roman Catholic Church rather than on that Church's involvement in the world in the cause of Justice and Peace. In a previous chapter I described how the Mass became important to me. Hand in hand with that came the realisation that the Church's social teaching is not gathering dust on a shelf, but is taking flesh in today's world. The active Justice and Peace groups are an effective sign of this.

Notes

[1] BBC1, *Everyman*, 3 May 1992

[2] Barr, James, *Fundamentalism*, SCM Press, 1981

[3] St Matthew 25:35–39, *Jerusalem Bible*, Darton, Longman & Todd

[4] St Matthew 25:40, *Good News Bible (Today's English Version)*, Bible Societies and Collins

[5] *Centesimus Annus*, Catholic Truth Society, 1991, pp.46, 47, 49

[6] Ibid., p.37

[7] Ibid., p.38

[8] Robinson, John A T, *Honest to God*, SCM, 1963, p.87

[9] Ibid., p.90

Galilee to Rome

A year before the 'intifada' erupted, I was able to fulfil a lifelong ambition by visiting the Holy Land. It was a pilgrimage with a difference; the party of which I was a member visited not only the 'holy places' but also met people of the land. Among these were Jews and Palestinians, Moslems and Christians.

Third-world shanty towns had been remote from my experience until we entered the Gaza Strip. The visit had been made possible by prior arrangement with the authorities, including representatives of the United Nations and the Red Crescent. As we met the deprived families in Rafah refugee camp, I felt a sense of shame for having allowed myself to accept the stereotype of the Palestinian as terrorist. The Israeli army gun towers surrounding the Gaza seemed reminiscent of the pictures I had seen in 1945 of their German equivalents around ghettos and concentration camps.

Despite our visit having been authorised, it ended abruptly. Two jeep-loads of trigger-happy Israeli soldiers roared down the dusty road towards our minibus. One male member of our party (a GLC councillor) turned pale and whispered to me, 'I don't think we are going to see London again!' After prolonged negotiations on the part of the UN representative, we were escorted out of Gaza at gunpoint. It was a mild foretaste of the Palestinians' everyday experience. The point of my narrating this sensational event from the Israeli–Egyptian frontier is that it served to sharpen my conviction that we may not separate the Christian gospel from issues of Justice and Peace.

But how does this relate to my Evangelical pilgrimage to Rome? When all is said and done, the Holy Land (and Jerusalem in particular) is itself a focal point of Christian disunity and discord pre-dating the Protestant Reformation by centuries. It is well known that the Church of the Holy Sepulchre (built over the most likely site of Jesus' death and burial, and 'shared' by six Christian Churches) is a continuing symbol of this disunity. In retrospect, my time in Jerusalem made a significant contribution to my later decision to become a Roman Catholic. Visits to the Christian holy places were coloured by what I had heard from others who had visited previously and who had complained of commercialisation. It came as a surprise, therefore, to find myself moved by the Roman Catholic shrines in particular, many of which are maintained by the Franciscans. These Franciscan shrines seem to have captured the authenticity of the saving events to which they bear witness, and to have achieved this in an aesthetically satisfying way and without tawdry embellishment.

On the western slope of the Mount of Olives stands the tear-shaped chapel of Dominus Flevit, its large window behind the altar giving a panoramic view of Jerusalem. Dominus Flevit marks the spot where Jesus wept over the city. The memory of that visit is a reminder of the pain Jesus felt in his heart by our half-hearted response to him and to our neighbour. Dominus Flevit might have been conceived as a dark and miserable place. Instead, the Franciscans have captured in that simple building not only the sorrow of Jesus but also something of the fresh perspective and new vision of the world that he brings us.

The sights and smells of the old walled city of Jerusalem are a culture shock to the western visitor. But the narrow streets and dark alleyways with their traders, jostling crowds and laden donkeys, form the most appropriate setting for the Friday 'Stations of the Cross'. As we joined the procession, it was the Franciscans again who led the way through the hubbub, along the narrow winding Via Dolorosa to the place where Jesus was crucified. Moving as it was to visit the Church of the Holy Sepulchre and ponder the evidence for that being the actual spot of the Cruci-fixion, the building and its artefacts failed to convey any 'feel' of the awful event that had taken place. Successive desecrations and rebuilding, together with the territorial infighting of the Churches, had left their mark. It all contrasted with the stark reality of the Franciscan procession through the 'souks' with their noisy bystanders.

At the foot of the Mount of Olives lies the Garden of Gethsemane and the Franciscan Church of All Nations. The garden is lovingly tended; among the olive trees is one that has probably been there since Jesus' night of agony. The Church of All Nations is so named because it was built with funds donated by Roman Catholics of all nations. The altar table stands over the visible outcrop of rock on which Jesus' tears and sweat of blood fell. The subdued blueish light of the Church's interior seems to express the Lord's anguish.

It was here on the late Thursday afternoon, as darkness fell, that we joined the weekly 'Holy hour' led by the Franciscans. With the Blessed Sacrament – the Sign of Christ's Presence – exposed on the altar, there were gospel readings in several languages, interspersed with short meditations and silence. Despite some untimely camera flashes from a few tourists, there was a profound sense of the Presence of Christ. A question began to arise in my heart and mind: is the exposed sacrament simply a symbol, or is the Risen Christ actually present on this altar as we focus on this solemn location? As I now reflect on that scene, I know the experience was no mere spiritual 'pick me up'; for that was the place not only of Christ's own emotional struggle, but also of his betrayal; a powerful reminder of the Judas in each human heart!

For those of us accustomed to motorways, Galilee seems a long way from Jerusalem. The main road winding its way through the hills of Samaria is more akin to main roads in remote parts of Scotland or Wales. By the lakeside is Capernaum, the headquarters of Jesus' work in Galilee. It was here, a Palestinian Christian told me, that Jesus conducted his free clinic. He expressed very aptly the close link between the gospel and healing. There has been increasing awareness of this in the Churches generally. In the Roman Catholic Church in particular, the sacrament of the sick (Holy Unction) has been always available. It always seemed to me that the Reformers were wrong to reject this sacrament because it had become generally regarded as a preparation for death. In the Roman Catholic Church today, the sacrament of anointing the sick is seen as the sign of spiritual strength and healing. The retrograde action of the Reformers is curious in the light of scriptural teaching.[1] I have myself received this sacrament, and have good cause to be thankful for its availability!

The excavations at Capernaum are particularly interesting, revealing harbour and warehouse installations of long ago, confirming that the place was once a thriving commercial centre. I began to thank God for the industrial chaplains' insights into Galilee, seeing it as the area of business and industry where Christ invites us to follow him. The excavations have also revealed St Peter's house, which later became a church. What I found even more striking was Simon Peter's landing place. The unspoilt landscape is probably much the same as in Jesus' day. There is a rocky promontory with ancient rock-hewn steps leading down to the water. This is likely to be the place where the Risen Lord reminded Peter of his commission and responsibility for the whole Church.[2]

One of the most significant events of the Holy Land pilgrimage was the meeting with Fr Elias Chacour in northern Galilee. Elias Chacour is a priest of the Melkite Church, which is in communion with the Roman Catholic Church. He is a Palestinian, from a Palestinian Christian family which has lived in the country for many generations and whose members have suffered greatly since the founding of the State of Israel. Elias Chacour has worked tirelessly for Justice and Peace, regarding Palestinian and Jew as brothers. One of his first acts on moving into his parish was to work for community harmony by rebuilding the mosque! He then went on to build an excellent secondary school, serving both Christian and Moslem students. There was no intention of excluding Jewish students; this is the only secondary school in a very large area open to Palestinians. Elias Chacour has had a hard struggle to achieve these objectives, and has received threats to his life. In attempting to assess the significance of this encounter in relation to my journey to Rome, perhaps it is this: Elias Chacour is just one of many pastors in communion with Rome, who, by their clear and courageous witness to Justice and Peace in places where their lives are at risk, demolish the false notion of the Catholic Church as an esoteric sect. I have used the phrase 'Justice and Peace issues', which sounds very impersonal. I have constantly to remind myself that each 'issue' represents human faces and suffering people.

Looking at the Holy Land experience as a whole, in relation to my coming into communion with the Roman Catholic Church, there appear to be two main threads running throughout. Wherever we travelled in Israel there was evidence of Israeli repression of the Palestinian people, ranging from loss of land rights to harassment and detention without trial. Against that dark background there stood out in sharp relief the reconciling work for Justice and Peace pioneered by Fr Elias Chacour. The other thread which will have been apparent is the impact made upon me by the holy places maintained by Roman Catholics and the Franciscans in particular. Here I lay myself open to the charge of 'emotionalism'. I admit to a large affective element in that experience; but then, God has created men and women as emotional beings. Over the years I have often heard the charge of 'emotionalism' levelled at both Evangelicals and Roman Catholics, and especially at Charismatics. I recognise that emotion can take over, at the cost of the mind and the will. The accusation of emotionalism is often brought by those churchmen who are very cerebral and suspicious of 'showing emotion'. It is important to keep in mind that emotional factors play a large part (perhaps the greatest part when unrecognised) in our human motivation. We are not simply cold, rational beings. The first and great Commandment recognises this affective dimension when it reminds us: 'Love the Lord your God with all your heart...' In criticising the emotional element in faith, we may be criticising genuine spiritual experience.

Notes

[1] James 5:14
[2] St John's Gospel 21:15–17

A Mental Map

O ne of the valuable things I was taught by psychiatrists in my mental-health training was to try to 'distance' myself from a human problem; that is, as far as possible, 'look at it' from outside myself. It is very difficult, perhaps impossible, to do this completely, for each of us is motivated by powerful emotions which drive us to respond almost automatically to one another. It is because the conditioned response is, more often than not, neither helpful nor appropriate to the other person's problem, that this distancing is so essential in counselling. Those who have either been patients or worked with psychiatrists will be familiar with that 'distant look'!

It is worth having a go at that distancing discipline when we think about the divided Churches and the relationship of Christians to each other and to Christ. This is what I have attempted in this chapter. It is inevitably subjective; that is to say, it is the way I perceive this pattern of relationships. For the same reason and for limitations of space it is inevitably selective. So my mental map may not commend itself to everyone. The reader's perception of the same complex situation may be quite different. My hope is that by sharing my mental map of the area, it may stimulate further thought towards that unity for which Christ prayed.

In the past I have thought in terms of a two-dimensional or straight-line model. I can best explain my meaning if I start with the Anglican 'Via Media' concept. Anglican theologians have often spoken of the Church of England as a Via Media, a middle way between the Roman Catholic

Church on one side and the various Protestant Churches on the other. This view has not been confined to a few abstract thinkers. Church of England clergy have traditionally spoken of Anglo-Catholics and Evangelicals as 'wings' or 'extremes' of their Church, with various shades in between meeting as 'central' churchmen.

In my youth, when ecumenical thinking in Britain was embryonic, there was a powerful tendency for Anglicans to view themselves as the 'proper Church' as distinct from the 'errors of Rome' on the one hand, and the 'disorder and ranting of Chapel' on the other! In short, the Church of England was seen as representing the middle road of orthodoxy and sanity! This view was, of course, as arrogant as some Roman Catholic attitudes of that time. I have no wish to rake up the dust of the past. However, to understand the strength of Anglican Via Media thinking, it is necessary not to lose sight of the luggage in the loft! Quite recently, a Church of England clergyman said at an ecumenical service: 'Do we Anglicans look to the right to Rome, or to the left to Methodism?' The rhetorical question was asked sincerely and not in a partisan manner. Nevertheless it implies a two-dimensional mode of thought: a mental map with the Church of England as the central reference point.

If we return briefly to the 'two wings' idea of the Church of England, we can see how the 'straight line' thinking is so persistent. The Anglo-Catholics think of themselves as 'nearer to Rome' than other Anglicans. Those in this category often style themselves as 'Catholics' to distinguish themselves from other Anglicans. This has always struck me as curious, for either the Church of England as a whole is 'Catholic' or none of it is. After all, the Church of England does value the 'Catholic creeds' among its official statements of belief.

An Irish Roman Catholic priest once asked me: 'Are yer

one of those who imitate us?' The questioner's tone made it abundantly clear that he regarded Anglo-Catholics as far removed from the Church of Rome as the rest of Protestants! There is an element of delusional thinking in the minds of those who adopt that Anglo-Catholic stance, for, as we shall note presently, in some respects the Quakers may be equally 'near' to the Roman Catholic Church.

Evangelical Anglicans, on the other hand, have not normally thought of themselves as 'near to Rome'; usually quite the opposite. Even in pre-Vatican II days, however, Evangelicals stood solidly with the orthodoxy of Roman Catholic belief in such matters as the truths enshrined in the creeds and biblical inspiration. They took equally seriously the atoning death of Jesus and the need of personal salvation; heaven and hell, Christian living and spirituality. Nor were fear and guilt far from the minds of both Evangelical and Roman Catholic preachers at that time. Obviously I am skating over the surface. There were sharp differences, some of which have received attention in other chapters. Following the changes implemented by Vatican II, Evangelicals and Roman Catholics are even closer. The vernacular, together with simplicity in ceremonial, are matters that have exercised Evangelical Anglicans in the past.

In trying to evaluate the notion of 'nearness to Rome', there is a risk of becoming preoccupied with outward things, and so missing the essential heart of Catholic Christianity. Anglo-Catholics have tended to become caught up in nineteenth century Roman Catholic practice and have fought to bring that practice into the Church of England. However, they lack the authority base of the Roman Catholic Church; they are still enmeshed in the structure of the Established Church. In consequence they have become lost in an ecclesiastical cul-de-sac. The Roman Catholic Church is a large supranational pilgrim community, and this implies struggle, movement and change. It struggles, however imperfectly, to respond to the ever-changing challenges of the real world.

We need, then, to move away from the two-dimensional straight-line model with its notion of 'wings' touching other bodies; a model that is stifling and too limiting. It may be more fruitful to think of the relationship between Christian Churches as being more accurately depicted by the world globe, by which many of us learned geography.

I can recall my surprise at discovering, by looking at a globe, how a great circle route could be the nearest route between two places on earth, whereas, on a two-dimensional map, the straight line appeared the obvious route. Think of a globe with its features made up of Christian Churches rather than continents or countries, and with Christ at its centre. Our global map should not be thought of in terms of the geographical areas covered by Churches, but simply as Christian communities marked as symbolic shapes on different areas of the surface. For simplicity's sake it may be easier to confine ourselves to those Christian communities that we recognise as Churches in Britain, or with which we are familiar. Obviously, it is impossible to fabricate an actual globe of this type within the confines of print, so I must ask you to use your imagination. Once we are away from the limitations of the two-dimensional map of inter-church relationships and think along the lines of the great circle routes, we can begin to think of these relationships in a new way. The various Christian bodies may be equally near to the largest Christian community – the Roman Catholic Church – at certain points, while being widely apart at others. If this seems too abstract, it may be worth considering one or two concrete examples. Neither the Salvation Army nor the Quakers celebrate the sacraments in the sense that these are understood by other Christian Churches. At this point, therefore, they appear to be distant from the Catholic Church. But in other respects they are closer than other 'mainstream' Churches in England. The Salvation Army model of authority closely parallels the Roman Catholic hierarchy, with a 'general' as the leader of this international body. Nor does its point of contact end with formal structure. From its outset, the Salvation Army has been committed to the gospel of 'wholeness': soap, soup and salvation! The social conditions of the nineteenth century that saw the birth of the Salvation Army, also contributed to Pope Leo XIII's Encyclical, 'Rerum Novarum', which pointed the way to social justice and peace. This has given inspiration to the powerful and practical movement for social justice that is so much a part of the life of the Catholic Church today. Catholic understanding of the gospel is holistic, like that of the Salvation Army; that is to say, it is concerned with material as well as spiritual issues.

Whereas the Salvation Army adheres to the 'Evangelical' understanding of the gospel, the same cannot be said unreservedly of the Quakers. The Society of Friends, although a movement of Christian spiritual revival in origin, is a 'broad church', embracing both committed believers in Christ and those who can best be described as 'believers in God'. The members are not, in other words, obliged to accept the creeds. Some may therefore question my reference to the Quakers, for at first sight they appear to form an island very remote from the Catholic continent!

However, the great circle model may well allow us to see that the Quakers are nearer to the Roman Catholic Church at some points than many may suppose. It is too easy to focus on the absence of sacraments as such and to allow this to blind us to Quaker spirituality.

A member of the Society of Friends once said to me: 'Our Meeting for Worship, centreing on God, can be thought of as a Eucharist without bread and wine!' The idea of a Eucharist without bread and wine may seem inconceivable, but try to hold on to the suggestion just for a moment. The most striking fact of a Quaker Meeting for Worship is its positive silence, which can last for the whole hour. There is no sense of time dragging or embarrassment, but of centreing on God. The nearest experience to that quality of silence that I have known is a Catholic 'hour of prayer'; united silent prayer before the exposed Blessed Sacrament. Gerald Priestland, writing from a Quaker viewpoint, says: 'The Catholics, in particular, do understand that silence is the very heart of prayer.'[1] I have found an economy in the use of words in both Quaker worship and Catholicism. Both contrast with the average 'nonconformist' service, and indeed many Anglican ones, which all too often seem to depend upon a torrent of one-way communication as a hallmark of validity. The Quaker writer, Harvey Gillman, makes an interesting comment: 'I once met a Benedictine monk who was interested in the Religious Society of Friends. His problem was that he was tired of the repetition of words. This monk and I agreed that it would be nice if there could be a sort of silent mass.'[2] Quakers come to their Worship Meeting to bring their life experience into their centreing on God. Could there be a parallel here with the offertory at Mass?

There is another area shared by Catholics and Quakers which is significant for today's world. Both take seriously Christ's words: 'Inasmuch as you did it to... you did it to me.' The Quakers have believed since their inception that something of God may be found in every person. They put it in the quaint phrase: 'That which is of God in every man.' Harvey Gillman, elaborating on this, says: 'Quakers share with other mystics the insight that God can be found in the everyday experience of all people ... One monastic tradition which I find very appealing is the law of hospitality; each guest is Christ at the door waiting to come in. At this point the Catholic and the Quaker traditions are very close, for the holy is part of ordinary experience, the guest and Christ are one when seen with the eyes of faith and compassion.'[3] The important feature of this shared Quaker and Catholic 'doctrine' is that it is not empty theory; the practical outworking is evident in all kinds of social service and peace issues by both communities.

I have devoted considerable space to the areas of proximity between Quakers and Catholics in order to illustrate the limited perception afforded by the linear model of ecumenism. There are, of course, many points of contact between other Christian Churches and the Catholic Church, and I leave the reader to reflect on these. I have focused on what may be considered two 'unlikely' bodies and less familiar meeting points, to illustrate the need for wider thinking. I almost said lateral thinking, but that might be confused with 'two-dimensional'!

My children used to have a world globe which was illuminated by an electric lamp at its centre. Not only did it serve its purpose as an aid to learning world geography, it also illuminated Christ's saying: 'I am the light of the world.'[4] Any light shining out through Christian communities comes from Christ; from Christ, the centre of our being.

_____

Notes

[1] Priestland, Gerald, *Reasonable Uncertainty: A Quaker Approach to Doctrine*, Quaker Home Service, London, 1992, p.15

[2] Gillman, Harvey, *A Light That Is Shining: An Introduction to the Quakers*, Quaker Home Service, 1988, p.28

[3] Ibid., p.14

[4] St John's Gospel 8:12, *Jerusalem Bible*, Darton, Longman & Todd

Question Time

Some ten years have passed since the foregoing chapters were written, giving opportunity to reflect upon their content and whether they adequately portray the development of my thinking. Since then, I have retired and moved to a different Catholic parish.

One of the important lessons I have learned from my training and experience in mental health (which involved working closely with experienced psychiatrists) was to take seriously one's first impressions of any new situation. These first perceptions are often of greater validity than the habituated perception of people who have become accustomed to the given situation.

Some of the foregoing chapters reflect the first impressions of a 'new boy' in the Catholic Church (as one seasoned Catholic described me!). Nevertheless, these perceptions of the 'new boy' may be of value, not only to those non-Catholics who still retain the caricature of the Italian mission, but also to Roman Catholics where familiarity has bred, if not contempt, then lethargy.

There is, of course, the danger that the 'new boy' will be seen by his former colleagues as having accepted uncritically the 'Roman package'. There can be no repression of our critical faculty, for, as the first and great commandment requires – 'Love the Lord your God with all your mind' – all Christians are called to intellectual honesty. Again, it was in the psychiatric context that my critical faculty was sharpened. I worked with staff and patients, many of whom only a few years earlier had experienced a culture of intimidation, repression and violence. Many patients had become passively dependent upon the institution, their initiative sapped. Any large institution (secular or sacred) will tend to develop a resistance to change. It was all too easy for the hospital chaplain to accept unquestioningly whatever practices prevailed in the hospital. A group of lay people from a church in the hospital's catchment area had been visiting friendless patients on a long-stay ward for a year or more. One day the visitors found the ward locked. 'Why?' they asked. 'These people are our friends.' When that question was put to the consultant responsible, it was discovered that there had been no valid reason for depriving thirty patients of their liberty. To question accepted practice can lead to liberation of the captives. It may lead to souls estranged from the church finding the freedom Christ promises in the gospel.

If some of the protagonists of Christian Church history had put searching questions to their opponents instead of uttering condemnations, our sad divisions might have been avoided. If, today, Evangelicals were to take a fresh look at the role of Peter in the New Testament Church, approaching scriptural evidence with a question rather than seeking proof-texts to support the tradition of the Protestant Reformers, a different answer may become apparent. Certainly it has been so in my experience.

A question which Evangelicals tend to skate over concerns the nature of the Church. Their primary concern is that the gospel of salvation should be proclaimed; a once common catchphrase was 'every church an evangelising centre'. That was no doubt a laudable aim, but for those who took it seriously the denomination of the local church was of little consequence. What mattered was Bible-based teaching and the preaching of personal conversion to Christ. The underlying concept was (and is) that of the invisible church, the body of all true believers as distinct from the ecclesiastical communities of professed Christians. The different forms of ministry are seen simply as different management structures. To those who cling on to this view, I have to ask – are you sure that such is the church of the apostles? Moreover, are you not confusing the Church with the kingdom of God?

Another unresolved question confronting Evangelicals (as it confronted me) concerns the true understanding of our Lord's words at the Last Supper with the twelve Apostles. For many years it seemed to me that our Lord's words would always remain open to ambiguity. When he broke the bread, saying, 'This is my body', and over the cup of wine, 'This is my blood', did he intend those words to be taken literally (as in the Catholic understanding) or symbolically (as generally understood by the Evangelicals)?

Given the clear command – 'Continue to do this in memory of me' – ambiguity would be out of character. So who decides which is the correct understanding? When Christian leaders themselves are divided in their understanding, someone has to make a final decision as to what is right. It is in questions such as these that the Pope (as Peter's successor) exercises that same authority given by Jesus Christ to St Peter. Sadly, when that authority is rejected, the alternative (as history has demonstrated) is endless controversy resulting in schism and sectarianism.

I was compelled to ask myself whether I had grasped the full meaning of the word, translated into English as 'memory': Do this in *memory* of *me*.[1] This keyword in the Greek New Testament is *anamnesis*, which means 'to call to mind'. The question then arises, whose mind? Evangelicals immediately reply, 'Our minds of course; God needs no reminder.' I began to question this assumption in the light of its usage in Scripture.

When God makes the covenant with Noah and his sons, giving the rainbow as the sign of that covenant, God says,

'When the rainbow appears I will see it and *remember* the everlasting Covenant between me and all living things on earth.'[2] The word used in the Greek translation of the Hebrew Old Testament is that same word used by Jesus at the Last Supper. Here the 'Remembering' is objective and concrete, not just a psychological remembrance but one with God's action in salvation.

Similarly, in the Benedictus the song of Zechariah following the birth of his son John the Baptist, it is God who *remembers* his holy covenant.[3] Again, the same Greek word used by the Evangelist to record the Aramaic words of Jesus at the institution of the Eucharist.

'In scripture, when God remembers, it never means a mere recollection on the part of God, but when God remembers somebody he acts. He grants his grace, he fulfils his promise.'[4] 'In the anamnesis the Church calls to mind the Passion, Resurrection and glorious return of Christ Jesus, she presents to the Father the offering of his Son which reconciles us with him.'[5]

For Evangelicals, however, any suggestion that we may be re-offering the sacrifice of Christ is understood to conflict with the one perfect and complete sacrifice on the Cross, which is emphasised in the New Testament letter to the Hebrews.[6] There we see that in contrast to the sacrifices of the Old Covenant, which were repetitive, Christ's sacrifice had been offered once for all time. When I began to attend Mass, there were two sections of the rite that troubled me: the response of the congregation at the offertory – 'May the Lord accept the sacrifice at your hands'; and the striking language of the first Eucharistic prayer – 'We pray that your angel may take this sacrifice to your altar in heaven.' Was there not conflict here with the teaching of the scripture? It was at this point that the *Catholic Commentary on Holy Scripture* has come to my aid. ' "What then of our Masses?" one may ask. The answer is that they are only the one sacrifice of Christ perpetually commemorated, re-presented, applied to our daily needs, individual and social.'[7] As the more recent *Catechism of the Catholic Church* puts it: 'In the liturgical celebration of these events, they become in a certain way present and real.'[8]

An instance of the Reformers' overreaction lies in their treatment of Holy Unction. During my years in the Anglican Ministry I drew attention to the anointing of the sick as taught by St James.[9] Sadly, this was seldom requested, for from the Reformation until the twentieth century there was no provision made for its use. The Reformers rejected the sacrament on account of its having become Extreme Unction in Medieval practice. The question remains: why did not Archbishop Cranmer and his successors restore Holy Unction to its rightful place as the sacrament of the sick? I am very thankful for the unambiguous faith and practice of the Catholic Church, having received this sacrament both before major heart surgery and following a minor stroke.

Questions may create discomfort, even feel threatening. Jesus' challenging questions to the Jewish establishment created such a sense of threat to the security of their system that it led to his torture and death. The Second Vatican Council, convened by Pope John XXIII, questioned accepted attitudes and practice. It is healthy for the Church to face such questions: the Church is then in a stronger position to question the world's values.

In an age of abortion on demand, the Catholic Church gives a clear witness to the sanctity of life. In contrast to this unswerving witness, many married Catholics question the ban on contraception. If this questioning stems from the *sensus fidei* of the body of the faithful,[10] should it be swept aside? Malta is proud to describe itself as a Catholic country. Older Maltese women, however, who have endured poverty, recall being told in the confessional that they would only be given absolution if they were to promise to have more children. Such direction contributed to a climate of poverty and deprivation for these children. Should not the last word for a married couple lie not with the confessor but with their conscience? Can it be that the fundamental belief in the God-given value of human life and its transmission has become codified in an unhelpful rigid law?

It appears that a similar culture to that of Malta still prevails in parts of Latin America, leading to the grim situation of the 'street children', many of whom are (reportedly) shot by the police. Can we, as Catholics, truthfully say that there is no connection whatsoever between such terrible actions and the Church's 'ban' on contraception? Clearly it would be irresponsible and foolish to attribute responsibility for such evils solely to the 'ban' – the ills of Latin America stem from the deeply rooted injustices resulting from the unequal distribution of wealth and land. Nowhere do we see this highlighted more clearly than in the life and martyrdom of Archbishop Oscar Romero of El Salvador. Oscar Romero lived his life amid the poverty and injustice of Latin America. As Archbishop of San Salvador, he became a man of the poor, their advocate when they had no other voice to demand justice for them. He suffered and gave his life on their behalf.[11] He was shot in 1980 while celebrating Mass.

It was as I pondered the life and death of Oscar Romero that a further question presented itself. While he was loved and respected by the priests of his diocese and their poor parishioners, he did not enjoy the wholehearted support of the papal nuncio, this despite his loyalty to Pope Paul VI, the teachings of Vatican II and the policies of the Latin American bishops at Medellin. Time and again it becomes apparent that the nuncio identified himself with the wealthy class and their oppressive government, a government allegedly responsible for disappearances, torture and assassinations of priests and lay people. The question arising from that tense situation is whether we are looking at a problem peculiar to a particular nuncio and local to El Salvador, or a wider structural problem. Does the 'diplomatic structure' (with its nuncios) create a kind of parallel hierarchy to that of the bishops? The bishops of the Catholic Church function in loyalty to the Pope; they are themselves the eyes and ears of the papacy by virtue of their involvement in the life of various nations. Why, therefore, is there need today of this further diplomatic layer?

When the General Synod of the Church of England made the decision to ordain women priests, a number of clergy decided to become either Roman Catholics or Orthodox. Although Pope John Paul II made it clear that the ordination of women to the priesthood was not the way forward in the Catholic Church, I found myself asking 'why not female permanent deacons?' While it is true that the first deacons were male, it is significant that their primary function was not liturgical but one of social administration.[12] When those first deacons were appointed by the Apostles, it would have been socially unacceptable in that first-century society for women to have carried out those responsibilities. Our social milieu is very different from that era. Women occupy all manner of responsible posts, which only a short time ago would have been denied them. I recall my own great surprise at meeting a young woman working as an engineer on the construction of the Channel rail tunnel! I am equally surprised by the apparent absence of a feminine voice at the higher decision-making levels of the Roman Catholic Church. The cardinals are all male, but there was a time when priests and deacons served as cardinals assisting the then Pope, so why not admit women to the diaconate, and 'elevate' some as cardinals today? This is not a trivial question when we consider that it was a woman, St Mary Magdalene, who drew the attention of the Apostles to the empty tomb.[13]

It was a great joy when I first attended Sunday Mass to discover that Holy Communion was administered in both kinds and moreover by both male and female Eucharistic ministers. All the more surprising, then, to find that the norm in Maltese churches was otherwise. In the light of the Council fathers saying 'Holy Communion considered as a sign has a fuller form when it is received under both kinds'[14], why is this not being realised in all the Churches? Is this a symptom of a deeper malaise, namely that decrees of the Second Vatican Council are not being fully implemented? 'Together with their head the supreme Pontiff, and never apart from him, the Bishops have full authority over the universal Church.'[15] Thus the Council stressed the collegial authority of the bishops, in communion with the Pope. When considering the Roman curia, the fathers of the Council stressed that its departments should be reorganised and modernised.[16] There does seem to be a feeling at 'ground level' that the Roman curia is a powerful institution with an authority of its own. My only remaining question is whether the Council fathers' recommendation is taking full effect? In this chapter my aim has been neither to make accusations nor to level criticisms, but to raise some unresolved questions, some of which are addressed to Evangelicals, others to Roman Catholics. The questions are raised not primarily to satisfy an academic curiosity but in the hope that they may contribute to a better understanding and greater sharing of faith between Catholic and Evangelical Christians.

Notes

[1] St Luke's Gospel 22:19, *Good News Bible (Today's English Version)*, Bible Societies and Collins
[2] Ibid., Genesis 9:16
[3] Ibid., St Luke's Gospel 1:72

[4] Jeremias, Joachim, *The Eucharistic Words of Jesus*, Blackwell, Oxford, 1955, p.160 ff

[5] Chapman, Geoffrey, *The Catechism of the Catholic Church*, Cassell & Co, 1994, para.1354

[6] Hebrews 9 and 10

[7] *A Catholic Commentary on Holy Scripture*, Thomas Nelson & Sons, 1953, p.1169

[8] Chapman, op. cit., para.1363

[9] Epistle of St James 5:14–15

[10] Chapman, op. cit., paras.91–93 and First Epistle of St John 2:20

[11] Brockman, James R, *Romero: A Life*, Orbis Books, New York, 1989, p.ix

[12] Acts of the Apostles 6:1–6

[13] St John's Gospel 20:1–3

[14] Flannery, Austin, OP, [ed.] *Vatican Council II: The Conciliar and Post-Conciliar Documents*, Dominican Publications, Dublin & Talbot Press, Ireland, 1975, p.121

[15] Ibid., p.375

[16] Ibid., p.568

Conclusions

When in the 1950s I was trained for the Church of England Ministry at the London College of Divinity (now St John's College Nottingham), there was a great gulf between the Roman Catholic Church and ourselves. The only contact I and my fellow students experienced with the Catholic Church was an occasional visit to a Tridentine Mass or Benediction. Such visits were neither required nor made in response to any invitation; there was simply no personal contact. The London College of Divinity provided a thorough grounding in biblical theology. Although students were encouraged, or rather constrained, to approach their studies with an open mind, this was nevertheless undertaken within the received framework and ethos inherited from the Protestant Reformers.

We were trained in homiletics by none other than the late Dr Donald Coggan (our then Principal, later to become the Archbishop of Canterbury). It is perhaps not surprising that on the rare occasions I had the opportunity to hear Roman Catholic sermons, they seemed dogmatic and devoid of any scriptural reference. What a contrast with today's homilies, with their scriptural exposition and down-to-earth application. Contemporary Catholics are indeed fed from the table of the Word of God.

Following our ordination, my colleagues and I launched into the work of Evangelical pastoral ministry with commitment and enthusiasm. I am intrigued by the Vatican II document which quotes St Paul's moving words – 'woe to me if I do not preach the Gospel' – for this sentence was also the motto of my college and was taken seriously! Speaking of the lay apostolate, this Vatican II document stresses the need to reveal Christ to those around us both by our lives and by word. 'It is a fact that many men cannot hear the gospel and come to acknowledge Christ except through the laymen they associate with.'[1]

At the outset of my own ministry, however, were two residual doubts: the question of the 'Establishment' of the Church of England, and the non-Catholic understanding of our Lord's commission to St Peter.[2]

If the Vatican Council II and its reforms had occurred a decade or two earlier, I think it highly likely that I should have taken the step very much earlier. I have sometimes asked myself (and God) why Vatican II had to wait until the 1960s, but then I realise that is a pointless question, merely repeating the eternal 'why'. History does not revolve around me, much as I might wish that to be so!

I recall that, as a young Christian, after the famous broadcast sermon on conversion (to which I referred in my introduction), I promised that if and when the Roman Catholic Church displayed more evidence of Evangelical faith, I should join it. If that sounds arrogant, then my only excuse is the arrogance of youth! Changing personal circumstances in more recent times have provided an opportunity to look again, and more carefully, at the Catholic Church. I have been surprised with joy at the way in which the Holy Spirit has guided Peter's boat. Not least has been the reinterpretation and presentation of the Pope's status. No longer is Peter's successor carried around to demonstrate his importance. Instead, this servant of the servants of God prostrates himself and kisses mother earth.

I am persuaded that the Roman Catholic Church is committed to the gospel of Jesus Christ. It would be wrong to imply or infer that this commitment dates only from

Vatican Council II. Rather, it has become clearer since Vatican II, when many unhelpful accretions were cleared away. Because Christ has promised to guide the Church into truth under the leadership of Peter and his successors, it is able to 'unpack' the gospel to meet the changing challenges of the world.

In questions of belief, Evangelicals go back to the scripture, which on the face of it is right and laudable. In practice, however, this often means back to the institutionalised beliefs of the Protestant Reformers, regarded as an infallible authority. This often prevents Evangelicals from an open-minded reconsideration of the New Testament in relation to the Roman Catholic Church. They are more likely to become involved in discussion of Calvin or charismatic gifts than a serious reappraisal of Peter's primacy!

It used to be believed (and I suspect that it is still believed) by many non-Catholic Christians that Catholicism offers salvation by 'working your passage' to heaven, or, as sometimes put, 'by scoring Brownie points'. The reality is very different. The gospel of free grace runs like a thread through Catholic preaching. I could cite countless examples, but one must suffice. A visiting priest presiding at Mass used a phrase I have heard at many Evangelical rallies: 'Salvation is a free gift!' This really is the belief and teaching of the Roman Catholic Church, as (for instance) set out in Fr Herbert McCabe's *Catechism* and endorsed by imprimatur. I quote the relevant question and answer: 'Are we saved by faith?' We are saved by a living faith which is the free gift of God which we cannot deserve by any works or merit of our own.[3] It is sometimes said by Evangelicals that Roman Catholics lack Christian assurance. It is true that the New Testament promises: 'No one who believes in him [Jesus] will be condemned.[4] There can be no absolute guarantee, however, that we as humans, to whom God has given free will, will choose to continue on the hard road of discipleship to the end. Grace is freely offered but not forced upon us. Christ himself cautions us: 'Whoever holds out to the end will be saved.'[5]

Catholicism recognises itself as a community of sinners, each of whom is of great value to God. The Church accepts each person as (s)he is, not as an idealised or false projected self. This contrasts with the all-too-common expectation in Evangelical circles that conversion automatically brings twenty-four-hour unbroken sinlessness and happiness. Catholicism recognises that life is a struggle. Problems often arise when non-Catholics (and Evangelicals in particular) become sucked into the whirlpool of Calvinism. The practice of the Catholic Church can preserve Christians from this trap, which can consume so much energy. It is a nasty fact of life that baptised, believing Christians do fall into sin. In other words, we fall short of Christ's standards and likeness. And society's attitudes to right and wrong can either dull, distort or inflame our conscience. The ministry of reconciliation in the Catholic Church comes to our aid at this very point. However, I realise how difficult it is for those who have been socialised and warned against the supposedly 'evil system' of the Catholic confessional to readily accept this. There is no question of the priest acting instead of God, or coming between a person and the Lord. The best description I have heard of the ministry of reconciliation is: 'In the reconciliation room there are three of us; the priest, the penitent and Jesus!' Central to this sacrament is that change of heart of which the Catholic preacher of conversion spoke, all those years ago.

In the reconciliation room (where the unacceptable find acceptance) there is less chance of 'papering over the cracks' as may be the case in total reliance upon general confession.

It will have been apparent from the chapter entitled 'Mary' that, as a result of my first experience of the rosary, I developed an antipathy to its use. It was rushed, repetitive and strange; above all, to me at that time, it seemed wrong, the focus of the prayer appearing to be Mary and not Jesus Christ. To the uninitiated this seems a reasonable assumption, when ten 'Hail Marys' are offered in relation to one 'Our Father'. I now realise that in the rosary (one way of prayer), we are invited to meditate on a series of saving events of God's revelation in Jesus Christ, from the Annunciation to Pentecost. All these events (with the exception of the Assumption) are recorded in scripture. As we reflect upon each of these mysteries we bring to the Lord in company with Mary, our needs and the needs of others. Rather than simply repeating a list of names, those persons, those intentions, are brought into the saving gospel events. There are times when I still find the repetition difficult; then I recall the memory of some Evangelical prayer meetings where one participant has followed another with almost identical extempore prayers. As with all prayer, the searching question is whether that prayer is offered from heart and mind as well as with the lips.

The chapters on the Mass and the Real Presence described observable differences in the worship and atmosphere of Catholic and Anglican churches. Underlying this is a different approach to spirituality. As we have seen, Mass in the average Roman Catholic parish today is not the highly ritualised ceremony common to Anglo-Catholic churches. There is often an outward informality more reminiscent of a lively Evangelical-Anglican parish. Under-lying this apparently casual approach to worship, however, is a Christ-centred objectivity. Christ is present inde-pendently of the worshippers' feelings. Christ is there not only in the hearts and interpersonal relationships of the congregation, but present as the bread of life, independently of the strength and weakness of individual faith, just as he himself promised. This objectivity contrasts with the general tenor of non-Catholic worship, where there is an emphasis upon withdrawal from the ordinary material world to find God. Many then feel they are not being sufficiently spiritually minded, especially when small children are present and felt to be a distraction. This different approach to spirituality becomes apparent during the Eucharistic prayer in Catholic and Anglican churches. Whereas the majority of Anglicans shut their eyes, it is common for Catholics to pray with eyes open, deliberately watching and praying – with the Eucharistic action. I came to value the authenticity of the Catholic approach to spirituality not from arguments based on 'tradition' but from the teaching of scripture. When, for example, Jesus says, 'I am with you all the days,'[6] he does not qualify this by adding, 'but only on good days', or 'when you develop sufficient faith and mystical insight'!

One of the strengths of Evangelicalism is its emphasis upon daily Bible reading. The intention is to feed the time of personal prayer by meditation on the selected passage of scripture, rather than the pursuit of academic knowledge. Rather more difficult for those trained in vocal prayer is the prayer of silence. It is here that the Catholic practice of Exposition of the Blessed Sacrament comes to our aid. It provides the focus not only for supplicatory or intercessory prayer, but also for Adoration and Contemplation. As the Curé d'Ars, Jean-Baptiste Vianney replied, when asked why he spent so long before the Blessed Sacrament, 'I look at him and he looks at me!'

The experience of the Prophet Elijah on Mount Sinai is a well-known story from the Old Testament history. Elijah experienced the presence of God, not in the earthquake, wind or fire, but in the 'Sound of Silence'.[7] In the powerful silence before Benediction, when our talking to God ceases, the words of the Evangelical hymn have never been more timely: 'Be still, for the presence of the Lord, the Holy one, is here!'

In the chapter on the Real Presence of the Risen Jesus in the Eucharist, I referred to the wrong thinking that led some to view Christ as 'the prisoner of the Tabernacle'. If some Roman Catholics think of Christ in this way, how many non-Catholics construct other ways of imprisonment? The danger of trying to restrict the Lord's sphere of activity is by no means exclusive to Catholicism. It is just as easy to lock Christ into the pages of a favoured translation of the Bible. It is all too tempting to confine the real activity of Christ to our particular group or type of Christian experience. The subtlest temptation is to confine Christ to the 'spiritual' or 'religious' sphere, and so exclude him from those areas of life (social, business, professional) where his presence would demand change: not least in the power structures where we have influence. The corrective to such limited vision comes from St Paul when he says: 'Christ fills the whole universe with his presence.'[8] This in no way diminishes either Christ's Real Presence in the Eucharist or his speaking to us through scripture. I now joyfully accept the Roman Catholic understanding of the Eucharist as the sacrament of the presence of Christ. At the same time I am constantly challenged to discover Christ in my neighbour, not least in the poor and underprivileged.

As we have seen, the Roman Catholic Church is a pilgrim community. Considering the nature of the changing terrain its members have had to negotiate during the last forty years, it would be surprising if there were no stragglers. In the 1950s it was tempting for Catholics to use their faith as a shelter from the storms of life, and hopefully from those of purgatory and hell. If other Christians feel like applauding themselves at this point, they would do well to recall that most non-Catholics were equally blinkered to issues other than those of Church business and personal salvation. For both, the temptation is to cling to past securities, to stay in our 'shelters'. One of our greatest perils is 'institutionalisation'. I first became aware of this evil when I joined the staff of a large psychiatric hospital. Until then, it was as if I had been part of a Church affected by the process but without being able to name the disease. I came fresh to the mental hospital scene, and I was able to see the terrible effects of institutionalisation upon those within the system. I met people who had not only suffered the trauma of a mental health breakdown, but had also become chronic as a result of the hospital system itself. Their remaining initiative had been sapped and they simply adapted to the routines required by the system.

My new experience became a kind of mirror to what had been happening within the Church I knew and loved best, the Church of England. I began to see with new eyes the pressures operating upon its clergy, the powerful social expectations shaped by England's history as much as by the gospel. We can look back with the wisdom of hindsight and see how our Churches have been affected and blunted by institutionalisation throughout their history. It is not so easy to be aware of the pressures now operating: this calls for considerable reflection, 'distancing', courage and willingness to change. In drawing the parallel between the psychiatric Therapeutic Community and the Priesthood of All Believers, I attempted to show how the former might have something to offer the Churches as well as psychiatry. The Second Vatican Council provided opportunity for the Holy Spirit to speak to the Catholic Church's institutionalism. Perhaps it was comparable to the way the Lord addressed the Churches in the opening chapters of the Apocalypse. The Church began to listen, and we must pray that it will continue listening to the Lord who leads us in pilgrimage. There are many prophetic voices in the Church, drawing attention to the structural evil in God's world, such as countries where social injustice has become endemic. There are, sadly, some reactionary Catholics still locked into the idea their salvation is something remote from their brother and sister's needs. In the chapter on conversion I cited Hans Kung's striking picture of the Church's conversion. His graphic language depicts Vatican II not as a one-off event but as the beginning of a process of renewal and change.

I am old enough to remember the time when Catholics and non-Catholics rarely spoke to each other about Christian faith, and never met for worship or shared evangelism. How times have changed! Yet in my area, where Anglicans, Methodists and Roman Catholics meet regularly, there is an Evangelical group which excludes itself. It can be very threatening for Christians from different Churches to meet. A series of local ecumenical meetings revealed some real differences; discussion of these aroused deep feelings, which proved painful. Nevertheless, those taking part agreed it had been a valuable experience.

When we take seriously the urgent task of evangelism, the importance of all Christians witnessing to Jesus Christ as the Way, the Truth and the Life become apparent. I well recall the member of the painting-and-decorating profession who (from the top of his ladder) engaged me in conversation about religion. 'There are lots of different religions: Church of England, Methodist, Catholic, Baptist, Salvation Army!' His list comprised Christian Churches which he saw as different religions; a sad commentary on our present state. Many of the differences are real and cannot be glossed over, which makes the work of genuine ecumenism the more urgent.

Antony Archer, a Roman Catholic Dominican who is critical of his Church's conduct in England, is equally critical of the Church of England. Following ARCIC discussions on the Eucharist, Antony Archer commented: 'On the basis of these, Archbishop Coggan [then Archbishop of Canterbury] began in 1977 to urge the introduction of intercommunion between the two churches before the achievement of formal union between them. In this way it would be possible to avoid an examination of the structure of Anglicanism and in particular that of legal establishment...'[9] Short cuts such as that advanced by the late Dr Coggan are not the way to reunion. There are differing standards of and approaches to spiritual discipline, to be taken seriously. Differences of belief attract deep feelings, which have to be acknowledged and worked through if Communion is to reflect community.

So where do we go from here, from this impasse of denominations? Evangelicals seem content with this situation, providing there is cooperation in evangelism and intercommunion. Evangelicals generally regard the true Church as the invisible collective of genuine believers, and denominational divisions as relatively unimportant. This notion of an invisible Church arises from a confusion of Church and Kingdom of God. The Kingdom (or activity) of God is often invisible, for God is often at work without our realising. But from the time of the Apostles, the Church has been a visible community. The notion of an invisible Church is a cover to justify the endless splitting into new sects. To continue along that road not only wastes resources but is also a stumbling block to folk such as 'my painter' and contrary to the mind of Christ, who prayed for our unity. The acceptance of divided denominations is now largely a form of institutionalisation. In origin there may have been quarrels, or genuine differences of interpretation, or simply 'different ways of doing things'. The divisions are accepted because people have become used to the situation: to alter the set-up would threaten the sense of security of everyone concerned. Sadly, the Churches have become more institutionalised than the mental hospitals.

Allowing that there were good reasons for the original 'break with Rome' by the Churches of the Reformation, is the division justified today and would such a split happen now? These are the questions I have asked myself. Whether others feel that my answers, as I have attempted to set them out, are satisfactory, I must leave to the judgement of the reader. It will be apparent that I find my experience as a Catholic Christian is in no way a contradiction of my Evangelical faith in Christ: it is a fulfilment. I have come into Communion with the Roman Catholic Church somewhat late in the day, after recognising the quality of its renewal, its Christ-centredness, and its commitment to the gospel's implications for both the individual and society. When considering disputed doctrines, I have appealed to Holy Scripture rather than the early fathers, as this is the final authority for Evangelicals.

In my introduction I mentioned the zeal of the convert being noted for its intolerance. I have become aware of an unexpected feeling of impatience that if I can travel this road, why cannot others do likewise! Then I recall just how long it has taken me to reach Rome. I begin to feel a little better about my intolerant spirit when I read St Luke's account of an incident involving (of all people) St John. 'Master,' said John. 'We saw a man driving out devils in your name, but as he is not one of us we tried to stop him.'[10] That intolerant apostolic attitude has been repeated time and time again in Christian history; sadly, Christ's response has largely gone unheeded. So, although I have to keep in mind that the Lord does not tolerate intolerance, this does not negate the leadership commission he entrusted to Peter. In the light of that, I can see no other way forward to that unity for which Christ prayed than in the recognition of the Pope as the Church's 'Peter' today: the chief pastor Christ appoints to lead the worldwide Christian community. But, in the light of St John's experience with the man who was 'not one of us', the least we can do is to co-operate in making Christ known, even if we cannot agree in conscience in every matter of faith.

Is such co-operation either practical or possible? A Roman Catholic Priest, Pat Lynch, writing about 'Evangelism and the Catholic Church' says, 'One of my greatest desires is that this book will create an informative bridge between the Catholic Church and evangelical Churches.'[11] In Bearstead, an ecumenical mission took place, led by the Archbishop of Canterbury. In terms of sharing together in evangelistic rallies it was successful. In terms of making one-to-one contact with non-churchgoers in their homes (in a dormitory area) it was less successful. One contributory factor to this shortcoming may have been reluctance on the part of Christians (and especially Catholics) to talk about their faith in everyday conversations. Fr Pat Lynch commenting on his experience, says: 'Many good Catholics say to me, "I'll stuff envelopes or lick stamps, I'll even hand out hymn books, but please don't ask me to talk to people about Jesus"... When new Christians are asked what drew them to the Church, the most common answer is "another person". To speak on a one-to-one basis we don't need to be theologians, all we need is to be ordinary.'[12]

The small stream of people entering the Church through RCIA (Journey in Faith) is an encouraging sign but, taking account of the number of practising Catholics, we might expect the number of enquiries to be greater. In New Testament days the whole Church was vibrant with a sense of urgency. Men and women turned from paganism as ordinary Christians were willing to talk about Jesus in the marketplace. In this respect, Catholics can learn from the confident witness of Evangelical Christians – provided the latter's boldness is tempered with sensitivity. Shortly after the Second World War, a French Catholic priest, Abbé Michoneau, published a book about the grim spiritual state of France, *France Pays de Mission*, translated into English under the title of *Pagan France*. Abbé Michoneau confronted the Church in France with the extent of unbelief in that country. In England we are only slowly awakening to the reality of what Pat Lynch describes as de-Christianised society: 'We all as individuals need to be constantly evangelised so that a de-Christianised Europe can be Christian again.'[13]

In the chapter on Mary, I drew attention to the Olympic stadium in the mind of the author of Hebrews, with the great company of supporters cheering on the struggling runners. The writer invites us to run the gruelling race of Christian discipleship 'looking to Jesus', who not only leads the way but also accompanies us. Hanging on the wall in my home is a shield, an enlarged 'Crusader badge' with its central cross and Greek motto: 'Looking to Jesus'.[14] It was in the evangelical culture of Crusaders that I learned what the crucifixion of Jesus had to do with me, living 2,000 years later, and to look towards the Risen Christ in personal faith.

Critics might dismiss that experience as adolescent pietism. But the message of the shield was never presented as an easy opt-out, and over the years, like every other disciple, I have struggled to work this out in real life. It has become a reference point in human problems and given meaning to life's experiences, for the context from which the motto is taken is one of conflict and struggle. The shield still hangs on my wall because it still expresses my faith, but now as a Christian in the Pilgrim Community of the Roman Catholic Church.

For both Evangelicals and Catholics, the Cross of Jesus Christ is central to their faith. In my youth, as a member of Crusaders, I also learned that Jesus died of a broken heart – literally, a ruptured heart. Moreover, he died of a broken heart in the deeper sense in which we use the term, bearing the weight of our faults, our sins. Crucifixion is usually a slow and agonising death. On that occasion, the Roman execution squad had to hurry things along to prevent a riot and further trouble from the Jewish leaders, so they broke the legs of the other two victims to ensure a quick death. When they came to Jesus, he was already dead, but one member of the squad (for whatever reason) thrust a spear into Jesus' side causing an emission of blood and water.[15]

In Scripture, the word 'heart' includes the physical organ, but is much more than that; it may be summed up as the 'inner self'. It is worth keeping this in mind as we visualise St Peter writing his first letter to the Church with the crucifixion still vivid in his mind, 'He was bearing our faults in his own body on the cross...'[16]

The Catechism of the Catholic Church describes the pierced Heart of Jesus as the chief symbol of his love for each of us.

> He has loved us all with a human heart. For this reason, the Sacred Heart of Jesus, pierced by our sins and for our salvation is quite rightly considered the chief sign and symbol of that love with which the divine Redeemer continually loves the eternal Father and all human beings without exception.[17]

For Catholics, the pierced Heart of Jesus is also seen as the source of the sacraments. This is how the Catechism puts it:

> The blood and water that flowed from the pierced side of the crucified Jesus are types of Baptism and the Eucharist, the sacraments of new life. From then on it is possible to be born of water and the Spirit in order to enter the Kingdom of God.[18]

Is there any valid reason, then, why Evangelicals may not join Catholics in the Divine Praises?

> Blessed be Jesus Christ true God and true man.
> Blessed be his most Sacred Heart.
> Blessed be his most Precious Blood.

As I entered St Peter's Church, Bearsted for the first time, my attention was immediately drawn to the Crucifix above the tabernacle, with the arms of the carved figure of Christ extended in welcome. A year later, at the Shrine of Reconciliation at Walsingham, I would hear (with renewed force and meaning) the familiar comfortable words – 'Come to me, and I will refresh you.'

At Walsingham, the invitation was to come to our welcoming Saviour really present in the most holy sacrament of the altar, as we awaited his Benediction.

During the parish mission at St Peter's (to which I referred earlier) a woman spoke of the contrast between the older preaching, with its emphasis on fear, and the contemporary rediscovery of the prodigality of the Father's love (Luke 15:20–24). There came also a fresh understanding of the real humanity of Jesus: 'He is indeed Lord, but also our Brother and Friend.' The hymn 'What a Friend we have in Jesus' is as true for Catholics as for Evangelicals.

I have taken my title from the final chapter of the Acts of the Apostles (28:14). The writer of Acts believed it important to include 'And so we came to Rome' as the climax of St Paul's missionary journeys. In using those same words I do not presume to compare my journey of faith to that of St Paul, the greatest Christian missionary. However, that short sentence does have personal significance, for it seems to sum up my journey as an Evangelical Christian to the Roman Catholic Church.

Notes

[1] Flannery, Austin, OP, [ed.], *Vatican Council II, Volume 1*, Dominican Publications, Dublin & Talbot Press, Ireland, pp.773, 781–2

[2] Matthew 16:16–19

[3] McCabe, H, OP, *The Teaching of the Catholic Church*, Catholic Truth Society, 1985

[4] John 3:18, *Jerusalem Bible*, Darton, Longman & Todd

[5] Mark 13:13, *Today's English Version*, Bible Societies and Collins

[6] Matthew 28:20, Author's translation

[7] 1 Kings 19:11–12, Author's translation

[8] Ephesians 4:10, *Today's English Version*

[9] Archer, Antony, *The Two Catholic Churches*, SCM Press, 1986, p.242

[10] Luke 9:49, *New English Bible*, OUP and CUP

[11] Lynch, Pat, *Awakening the Giant: Evangelism and the Catholic Church*, Darton, Longman & Todd, 1990, p.3

[12] Ibid., pp.134–135

[13] Ibid., p.1

[14] Hebrews 12:2

[15] For the forensic evidence, see Bernard, J H, *A Critical and Exegetical Commentary on the Gospel According to John (19:34)*, Edinburgh, T&T Clark, p.646

[16] 1 Peter 2:24, Jerusalem Bible

[17] Chapman, Geoffrey, *Catechism of the Catholic Church*, p.107, para.478

[18] Ibid., p.279, para.1225, p.279

Glossary

Agiornamento	Italian word meaning 'bringing up to date'.
Anamnesis	In the original Greek New Testament meaning 'memory'.
ARCIC	The Anglican Roman Catholic International Commission set up to explore areas of common faith held by the Anglican and Roman Catholic Churches.
CAFOD	Catholic Fund for Overseas Development.
Eucharist	The sacred meal in which the sacrifice of Christ is recalled.
Eucharistic Offering	The offering of ourselves in union with the sacrifice of Christ.
Gnostic and Gnosticism	For definitions, see pp.49–50.
Pre-Vatican II	The era prior to the Second Vatican Council (1960–63).
Post-Vatican II	The years following the Council.
PCC	Parochial Church Council. A legally constituted body in a Church of England parish.
RCIA	Rite for the Christian Initiation of Adults. Also used to describe the enquiry course for those wishing to know more of the Roman Catholic Church.
Ultramontane	Supreme Papal Authority

Lightning Source UK Ltd.
Milton Keynes UK
18 June 2010
155762UK00001B/12/P